A SONG OF STONE

STONE

A Novel

Iain Banks

Simon & Schuster

SIMON & SCHUSTER
Rockefeller Center
1230 Avenue of the Americas
New York, NY 10020

First published in Great Britain
in 1997 by Abacus

SIMON & SCHUSTER and colophon are registered
trademarks of Simon & Schuster Inc.

Manufactured in the United States of America

1   3   5   7   9   10   8   6   4   2

Library of Congress
Cataloging-in-Publication Data
Banks, Iain.
A song of stone : a novel / Iain Banks.
        p.   cm.
        I. Title.
    PR6052.A485S66   1998
823'.914—dc21   98-13076
                CIP

ISBN 0-684-85353-1
ISBN 0-684-85725-1 Signed Edition

To my parents

CHAPTER
ONE

Winter always was my favourite season. Is this yet winter? I do not know. There is some technical definition, something based on calendars and the position of the sun, but I think one simply becomes aware that the tide of the seasons has irrevocably turned; that the animal in us smells winter. Disregarding the imposed grid of our chronology, winter is something inflicted upon our half-world, something taken away from the land by the cold and cooling sky and the low and lowering sun, something that permeates the soul, and enters the mind through the nose, between the teeth and across the porous barrier of the skin.

A raw wind picks and stirs small spirals of leaves across the broken grey surface of the road and dumps them scattering in the cold puddles of water at the bottom of the ditches. The leaves are yellow, red, ochre and brown; the colours of burning in the midst of this damp chill. Some leaves remain on the trees overlooking the road; no ice rims the ditches' mean trickle, and on both sides of the plain the hills are free of snow under a mid-day sun within a wide slice of cloud-free sky. But still it feels like all autumn's past. Northwards, in the distance, a few mountains hide behind a grey besieging fleet of clouds. Perhaps there is snow there, on those peaks, but we are not allowed to see it yet. The wind comes from the north, pushing veils of rain down the hills towards us. Across the fields to the south – some trample-blonde and wasted, some harvested and earth-bare, a few pitted with craters – columns of smoke climb, shifted aslant by the freshening breeze. For a moment, the wind smells both of rain and burning.

Those around us, our fellow refugees, mutter and stamp their feet on the greasy surface of the road. We are, or were, a stream of humanity, a surge of outcast people, arterial and quick in this quiet landscape, but now something holds us up. The wind dies again, and on its ebb I smell the sweat of unwashed bodies and the scent of the two horses pulling our makeshift wagon.

You reach up from behind me and hold my elbow, squeezing.

I turn back to you, brushing a wisp of jet-black hair away from your brow. Around you are clustered the bags and chests we thought to take, stuffed with whatever we hoped might prove useful for us but not too tempting to others. A few more precious items are hidden within and beneath the carriage. You have been sitting with your back to me in the open carriage, looking back along our route, perhaps trying to see the home we left, but now you are twisting round on the seat, trying to see past me, a frown troubling your expression like a flaw in a statue's marble face.

'I don't know why we've stopped,' I tell you. I stand up for a moment, looking out over the heads of the people in front of us. A tall-bodied truck fifty metres ahead hides the view beyond; the road here is straight for a kilometre or so, between the fields and the woods (our fields, our woods, our lands, as I still think of them).

This morning, when we and our few servants joined the flow of people, carts and vehicles, it stretched unbroken out of sight both up and down the road; a continuity of the displaced, all moving, shuffling, eyes cast downwards, trundling from roughly west to vaguely east. I had never seen such a mass of people; a river of souls upon that road. They reminded me of childhood paper-people, outlines cut from compressed newspapers and then pulled out, all linked, all similar, all slightly different, all taking their shape from what has been removed and – fragile, flammable, disposable – by their nature demanding some suitable ill-use. We joined them easily enough, fitting in yet standing out.

Some noises come from ahead. They may be shouts; then I hear the dry crackle of small-arms fire, sparse and sharp in the resuming wind. My mouth becomes dry. The people around us – families, mostly, little groups of kin – seem to shrink in on themselves. I can hear a child crying. A couple of our servants, leading the horses, glance back at us. After a while, a new, closer smudge of smoke rises from beyond the tall truck ahead. A little later still, the queue of people and vehicles starts to move again. I flick the reins and the two brown mares clop onwards. The tall truck's exhaust gives up a cloud of smoke.

'Were those shots?' you ask, turning and standing and

looking past my arm. I smell your scent, the soap from your last bath this morning in the castle, like a floral memory of summer.

'I think so.'

The mares edge us onward. The smell of the truck's diesel fumes lies briefly across the wind. Tied, hidden, under the carriage there are six drums of diesel, two of petrol and one of oil. We left our vehicles in the castle yard, reckoning the horses and this carriage could take us further towards whatever safety's to be found than could the motors. There is more to that calculation than just miles per gallon or kilometres per litre; from all the rumours, and indeed from the little we've seen so far, working vehicles, and particularly those capable of going off-road, attract the attention of exactly those we are currently trying to avoid. Just so the castle, seemingly so strong, only draws trouble to it. I have to keep telling myself – and you – that we have done the best thing, leaving our home to save it; those no doubt already picking over it are welcome to what they can carry.

The smoke ahead of us grows thicker, comes closer. I think perhaps a more possessive, less protective soul than mine would have burned the castle, this morning, when we left. But I could not. It would, no doubt, have felt good to deprive those threatening us their stolen reward, but still I could not do it.

Uniformed men with guns – uniforms and weapons both various, irregular – are shouting at the tall truck ahead of us. It lumbers off the road and into the entrance to a field, letting those behind it pass on by. The column of refugees ahead, a stream of folk, all heads and hats and hoods and wobbling piled-up carts, stretches towards the horizon.

We come to the source of the smoke, and by that rising column, ours stops again. By the road there is a burning van;

it lies tipped in the ditch, not quite on its side; an open trailer behind it sticks its rear into the air, its contents spilled from beneath a dark tarpaulin. The van pulses with fire, flames spilling from its broken screen and windows, smoke bustling from its flung-open rear doors. Our fellow travellers, at least those on foot, bunch to the far side of the road as they pass it, perhaps fearing an explosion. More uniformed men are picking at the scatter of goods spilled from the van's trailer, oblivious to the nearby fire. Spread on the ditch-bank near the van, what looked at first like two more piles of rags are both bodies; one face down and one, a woman, staring up to the sky with wide, immobile eyes. A brown-black stain discolours her jacket down one side. You stand, looking, too. A pitiful, desperate moaning comes from somewhere ahead.

Then, beyond the smoke and flames and the van's tilted roof, where a luggage rack had broken free and spread bags, drums and containers across the coarse grass and stunted bushes there is movement.

It was there we saw the lieutenant first, rising from beyond the wreck's full bloody flames, her figure distorted by that rising heat as though through twisting water; a rock to foul the flow.

A shot comes from where the tall truck is, stopped at the gate leading to a field ahead, opposite the entrance to a forest track. People duck around us, the horses start momentarily and you flinch, but I am held by the gaze of the figure beyond the flames. Some more shots crack out, and I turn at last, gaze torn, to watch people stumbling from the tall truck, hands raised or on their heads as more men in uniforms herd them away, drop the tailgate with a thud and start to rummage through the vehicle. When I look back, you are seated again, and the uniformed woman I saw through the flames is stepping,

7

flanked by two of these irregular soldiers, to the door of our open carriage.

Our lieutenant (though I'll admit we did not think of her as such then) is of average build, but with an air of gracefulness about her movements. Her plain face is dark, nearly swarthy, her eyes grey under black brows. Her attire is composed of many different types of uniforms; her stained, scuffed boots come from one army, her torn fatigues from another, her grimy, holed jacket from yet one more, and her crumpled cap – sporting wings as part of its insignia – appears to have originated in an air force, but her gun (long and dark, sickle-shaped magazines neatly taped back-to-back and upside down) is spotlessly clean and gleaming. She smiles at you and tips her cap briefly, then turns to me. The long gun rests easily on her hip, barrel threatening the sky.

'And you, sir?' she asks. Her voice possesses a roughness I find perversely pleasant, even as my skin crawls at a buried menace in her words, a promissory threat. Did she suspect, did she foresee something even then? Did our carriage mark us out within that crowd, a jewel set in a baser band, appealing to the predator in her?

'What, ma'am?' I ask, as somebody screams. I glance away to see a group of the soldiers gathered around somebody lying on the roadside, a few metres in front of the burning van. The refugees file past this group as well, keeping well away.

'Have you anything we might want?' the uniformed woman asks, swinging lightly up on to the carriage's kick-step and – with another smile at you – leaning over to lift the edge of a travel rug with the muzzle of her long gun.

'I don't know,' I say slowly. 'What is it you want?'

'Guns,' she shrugs, glancing, eyes narrowed, at me. 'Anything precious,' she says to you, then uses the long gun's muzzle to peek under another rug across the carriage from where you sit, pale-faced, wide-eyed, staring at her. 'Fuel?' she says, looking at me again.

'Fuel?' I say. It crosses my mind to ask if she means coal, or logs, but I leave the thought unsaid, intimidated by her manner and her gun. Another sobbing scream comes from the small huddle of men ahead of the truck.

'Fuel,' she repeats, 'ammunition—' Then a shriek comes from the group of men clustered ahead of us (you wince again); our lieutenant glances in the direction of that awful wail, a tiny frown forming and disappearing on her face almost in the same instant as she says, '—medical supplies?' A look of calculation appears on her face.

I shrug. 'We have some first-aid material.' I nod towards the mares. 'The horses eat grain; that's their fuel.'

'Hmm,' she says.

'Lucius,' someone says from ahead of us. Our servant mutters something in return. Two men walk from the small group gathered on the road; one of the irregulars and the Factor from the village. He nods to me. Our lieutenant steps down from the carriage and walks to him, then stands with her back to us, head bowed, talking to the Factor. He glances up at us at one point, then walks away. The lieutenant returns, steps up again, pushing her cap back over her dun-coloured, scraped-back hair. 'Sir,' she says, smiling at me. 'You have a castle? You should have said.'

'Had,' I reply. I cannot help but glance back in its direction. 'We've left it.'

'And a title,' she goes on.

'A minor one,' I grant her.

'Well,' the lieutenant exclaims, gaze sweeping round her nearby men. 'What should we call you?'

'Just my name will do. Please call me Abel.' I hesitate. 'And you, ma'am?'

She looks, grinning, round her men, then back at me. 'You can call me lieutenant,' she tells me. To you she says, 'What's your name?' You sit, still staring at her.

'Morgan,' I tell her.

She remains looking at you for a moment, then slowly turns her gaze to me. 'Morgan,' she says slowly. Then another cry comes from the group huddled on the road. The lieutenant frowns and looks that way. 'Stomach wound,' she says quietly, two fingers tapping on the polished veneer of the carriage's door. She glances at the two bodies lying by the burning van. She sighs. 'Just first-aid stuff?' she asks me. I nod. She taps the buxom quilting on the inside of the door, then steps down and walks towards the group crouched ahead on the road. The knot of men opens, the soldiers making way for her.

A young uniformed man lies on his side in the centre of the group, hands clutched round his belly, shivering and moaning. Our lieutenant goes to him. She lays her long gun down on the road surface as she crouches, stroking the lad's head and talking quietly to him, one hand at his brow, the other doing something at her hip. She nods a couple of the others out of the way – they retreat – then bends down and kisses the young soldier full on the mouth. It looks a deep, lingering, almost passionate kiss; a string of saliva, caught in the sunlight slanting over the trees, connects them still as she pulls slowly away. Her lips have hardly left his when the pistol she has placed at the boy's temple fires. His head jerks as though kicked hard, his body spasms once then relaxes and some blood flicks up and out across the road. (I feel your hand on my shoulder, clutching at my skin through the layers of jacket, fleece and shirts.) The young soldier uncurls and flops loosely on to his back – mouth open, eyes closed.

The lieutenant stands promptly, shouldering her rifle. She spares the dead soldier a last look, then turns to one of those who had been clustered round the wounded lad. 'Mr Cuts: see he's buried properly.' She holsters the still smoking automatic pistol as she glances at the two civilian bodies lying by the burning van. 'Leave those two for the dogs.' She walks back to our carriage, shaking a grey kerchief out of a pocket and dabbing at her face, removing a few small spots of the youth's blood. She jumps up on to the step again, folding her elbows over the carriage door.

'I was asking about guns,' she says.

'I ha– I have a shotgun and rifle,' I tell her, my voice shaking. I glance up the road. 'We may need them for—'

'Where are they?'

'Here.' I stand slowly, and look down at the box beneath the coachman's seat. The lieutenant nods to a soldier I had not noticed on the other side of the carriage, who jumps up, opens the box, searches it and hauls out the oil-heavy bag in which I stowed the guns; he checks inside, then jumps back down.

'The rifle is not of a military calibre,' I protest.

'Ah. That'll mean it can't shoot soldiers, then,' the lieutenant says, nodding ingenuously.

I glance round in the direction we were travelling. 'For pity's sake, we don't know what we might meet further on—'

'Oh, I don't think you need to worry about that,' she says, climbing a step higher on the carriage and giving another nod. The same soldier who took the guns clambers up beside me again. He proceeds to search me, efficiently but not roughly, while the lieutenant alternately grins at me and smiles at you,

11

who look on, gloved hands clenched but visibly trembling. The soldier has a sour, almost fetid odour. He finds nothing he judges worth exhibiting, save the heavy bunch of keys I put into my pocket this morning. He throws them to the lieutenant, who catches them one-handed and looks at them, holding them up and turning them against the light.

'A mighty bunch of keys,' she says, then looks at me, inquiring.

'The castle's,' I tell her. I shrug, a little embarrassed. 'A keepsake.'

She rolls them clinking round her hand, then with a flourish pockets them in her torn jacket. 'You know, we need some place to hole up for a while, Abel,' she tells me. 'Bit of rest and recreation.' She smiles at you. 'How far is this castle?'

'It took us since dawn to get this far,' I tell her.

'Why did you leave? A castle ought to be protection, no?'

'It's small,' I tell her. 'Not very formidable. Not formidable at all. Just a house, really; it used to have a drawbridge, but now there's just an ordinary stone bridge across the moat.'

She makes a show of being impressed. 'Oh! A *moat* . . .' She draws smirks from the soldiers around her (and I notice for the first time how tired and beaten-looking many of them are, as some gather round us, some carry away the body of the young soldier and others start to usher the people behind us round our carriage and onwards down the road. Many of them seem wounded; some are limping, some have arms in frayed slings, some dirty bandages on their heads like grey bandanas.)

'The gate is not very strong,' I say, and feel that my words sound as lame as some of these grubby, motley soldiers. 'We were worried it would be sacked if we stayed and tried to hold out,' I continue. 'There were soldiers there; trying to take it, yesterday,' I conclude.

Her eyes narrow. 'What soldiers?'

'I don't know who they were.'

'Uniforms?' she asks. She looks slyly around. 'Any better than ours?'

'We didn't really see them.'

'What sort of heavy equipment did they have?' she asks, then when I hesitate waves one hand and suggests, 'Tanks, armoured cars, field guns . . . ?'

I shrug. 'I don't know. They had guns; machine-guns, grenades . . .'

'Mortar,' you say, gulping, startled eyes looking from me to her.

I put my hand on yours. 'I'm not sure about that,' I tell our lieutenant. 'I think it was . . . a rifle grenade?'

Our lieutenant nods wisely, seems to think for a moment, then says, 'Let's take a look at your castle, Abel, shall we?'

'It's easy enough to find,' I tell her. I glance back the way we've come. 'Just—'

'No,' she says, opening the carriage door and swinging her short frame up and in to sit across from you. She levers some bags aside to get more comfortable and places the long gun across her knees. 'You take us back,' she tells me. 'I always wanted to ride in a carriage like this.' She pats the plush surface of the seat. 'And a little local knowledge can be useful.' She fishes inside her jacket – some sort of dark, ceremonial thing, torn in a few places, stained and smudged with dirt – then pulls out a gleaming silver case, opening it and offering it to you and me. 'Cigarette?'

We each refuse; she takes out a cigarette then puts the silver case away.

'I don't think going back is a good idea,' I say, trying to sound reasonable.

13

She is taking off her cap, pushing a hand through her short, mouse-brown curls. 'Well, too bad,' she says, frowning to inspect something inside her cap and running one finger round the inside rim. 'Consider yourself requisitioned.' She puts her cap back on and glances up at me with a small cold smile. 'Turn the carriage round and head back there.' She pulls a lighter from a breast pocket.

'But it took us since dawn,' I protest. 'And that was with the flow. It'll be after dark—'

She shakes her head quickly. 'We'll put the trucks in front.' She flicks the skip of her cap. 'People get out the way for a truck with a machine-gun; you'd be amazed. It won't take too long.' She makes a delicate twirling motion with one finger as she lights her cigarette with her other hand. 'Turn around, Abel,' she says through a cloud of exhaled smoke.

The tall truck ahead of us has been driven into the field; its diesel fuel is being siphoned off. We turn round in the gateway and a couple of jeeps and two six-wheel trucks with camouflaged canopies drive out of hiding in the forest track opposite. The soldiers who investigated the remains of the burning van load petrol cans and plastic drums into the back of one of the trucks, which go ahead of us back up the road, into the stream of refugees, horns blaring, a soldier standing proud of the leading truck's cab where a machine-gun points out. The people part and scatter before the trucks like water round the bows of a ship; it is all I can do to keep up. The mares break into a canter for the first time that day.

One of their jeeps follows immediately behind us. It too has a machine-gun, mounted on a post behind the front seats. The second jeep remains behind; two of the soldiers and our servants will bury the young soldier and then follow us.

14

The carriage rattles, sways and shakes; the damp wind courses round my face, cold and quick. The carriage's shadow, wheels flickering, is thrown long and spindly across the verge by the watery sun. The lieutenant looks pleased, and sits cross-legged with the gun balanced against one thigh, her cap on a bag beside her, her hand absently pushing through her short char-brown hair. She smiles at us both in turn. You look up at me, put one gloved hand up to mine.

Behind us, the refugees close up again and continue on their way. The burning van in the ditch makes a noise like a distant cough and a dark blister of smoke rolls upward into the greying sky, joining the smoke from all the other burning vehicles, farms and houses across the plain.

CHAPTER
TWO

And so we are delivered to the castle. I had not thought to see it again so soon; in fact I half expected never to see it again. I feel foolish, like somebody who has bidden a long and heartfelt farewell to a dear friend at a station, only to discover that through some misunderstanding they are on the same train. Still, as the trucks turn off the main road, leaving the line of refugees behind, I wonder what welcome awaits us. I have been watching for smoke as we approach, apprehensive that the soldiers who appeared yesterday might have sacked our home and set it on fire. So far, however, the sky above the trees where the castle is shows only the grey clouds moving down from the north.

The lieutenant investigates the interior of the carriage while we drive, finding much that fascinates her. I look round as she discovers your jewel box, behind your feet; you bend and hold it to your breast but she prises it from your hands with a deal of soft clucking and gentle admonishment that breaks your grip, I believe, as certainly as her greater strength. She inspects each piece in turn, admiring a few against her breast, around her wrist or on her fingers, before laughing and giving them back to you, save for one small ring of white gold and ruby.

'May I keep this?' she asks you. The carriage jolts, clattering over a pothole and I have to look forward again; your head is pressed up against the small of my back as I pull on the reins, keeping the mares away from a line of holes along the road. I feel you nod to her.

'Thank you, Morgan,' the lieutenant says, and sounds well satisfied.

She seems to doze for the last few minutes (you touch me on the back, to get me to look, and there is a smile on your face as you nod at her, head bobbing slackly). I am not so sure; our lieutenant's face does not appear completely relaxed to me, the way people really look when they are genuinely asleep. Perhaps she is still watching us, tempting us, waiting to see what we shall do.

However that may be, now she rouses herself, looks around, asks where we are and pulls a small radio from her tunic. She talks briefly into it and the trucks ahead of us growl to a stop on the driveway. I pull the carriage up just behind; the jeep idles to our rear. We are perhaps a half kilometre from the entrance to the castle's drive, hidden round a bend beneath the damp dark skeletons of the trees.

'Is there a gatehouse?' she asks me quietly. I nod.

'Any other road or track avoiding the gatehouse?'

'Not for the trucks,' I tell her.

'The jeep?'

'I'd think so.'

She stands quickly, rocking the carriage, tips her cap at you then nods to me. 'You lead us. We'll take a jeep.' You glance fearfully at me and put your hand out to me. 'Kneecap,' our lieutenant says to one of the men in the jeep. 'You look after the horses.'

The lieutenant gives orders I do not hear to the men in the trucks, then swings into the jeep, taking the wheel herself. The fellow sitting in the passenger seat holds a drainpipe-diameter olive tube about a metre and a half long. I take it to be a rocket launcher. I am squeezed in the back between the metal post supporting the machine-gun and a fat, pale soldier who smells like a week-dead fox. Behind us, sitting on the rear lip of the vehicle, crouches a fourth soldier who holds the heavy machine-gun.

We take the narrow forest track, round the back of the old estate, beneath the small escarpment fringed with dripping evergreens. The overhanging trees and bushes in places form a tunnel around the track, and the soldier manning the machine-gun curses quietly, ducking as snagging branches try to wrest the gun from his grip. The track approaches the stream that feeds the moat. The bridge is rotten, too frail for the jeep, timbers skewed and loose. The lieutenant turns to me, a look of disappointment beginning to form on her face.

'We're close now,' I tell her, keeping my voice low. I nod. 'Just over the ridge; there's a clear view.'

She follows my gaze, then says quietly to the soldier at the machine-gun, 'Karma, take the gun. Let's go.'

It would seem I am included. We leave the jeep unmanned and the five of us – the lieutenant and I, the man with the rocket

21

launcher, the fat, pale soldier and the one she called Karma, who totes the jeep's machine-gun and several heavy-looking loops of belted ammunition – cross the bridge and scale the steep bank on the far side. From the top, through bushes, the castle and the nearer gardens are spread out. It is a fine vantage-point. The lieutenant takes out a pair of small field-glasses, training them on our home.

A brief shower comes upon us, the falling drops catching in one last slant of sunlight levered underneath the rain clouds billowing down from the north. I look at my home, as a golden shroud of wind and rain wraps round it, trying to see it as another might; a modest castellation, not large; age-smoothed, sitting prettily in a ring of water and surrounded by lawns, hedges, gravel paths and outbuildings. The ancient walls – once pierced only by arrow slots, long since remodelled to allow more generous windows – are the colour of honey, in that rose-red light. It looks peaceful; but still, for all that architectural delicacy, somehow too strong for these brutal, disrespecting times.

Steeped in all this indiscriminate barbarity, anything standing proud invites a razing, like some defiant shout which only draws the hands' attention still faster to the throat, to grasp that moving strand of air by which we hang from and on to life. The only persistence in these unleashed days is achieved through low denominations and banality; in uniformity if not in uniforms, like that shoal of the displaced we tried to become part of. Sometimes the lowest bow is the highest guard to offer.

For now, all is still about the castle; no smoke rises, no figures stalk its square of battlements; no flag flies above, no light shines and nothing moves. There are still a few tents on the front lawns; people from the village who'd suffered the attentions of armed bands before and had thought the proximity of the castle might guarantee a degree of safety. Some smoke rises slowly there.

I think the castle never looked so good to me as now, for all that one lot of pirates are in charge of it and I am being forced to help another band even more determined to have it for their own.

The grounds around it are another matter; even before the despoilings inflicted by our mongrel dispossessed – cutting wood for fires, digging latrines in our lawns – the fields, woods and policies were running down, going to seed, becoming neglected. We lost our estate manager two years ago, and I – only ever distantly interested in the running of the estate – could not find it in me to take his place. Thereafter, gradually, all the other estate workers were taken by the war, one way or the other, and nature, unrestrained, began to renew its old authority over the burden of our lands.

'There, at the stables,' the lieutenant whispers, over the noise of raindrops pattering through the foliage around us. 'Those two four-wheel drives.'

'Ours,' I tell her. We left them there, and the stable doors unlocked, knowing that to attempt to secure anything would only invite more damage. 'Although we didn't leave the doors open like that.'

'That building with the slatted sides at the back of the garages,' the lieutenant says. 'Is that a generator house?'

'Yes.'

'Any fuel for it?' She looks at me hopefully.

Only under our carriage. 'The tank ran dry last month,' I tell her, truthfully enough. Saving our last few drums of diesel, we have mostly used candles for light and open fires for heating since then; the kitchen stoves burn wood too. There were fires and lamps that ran off propane, but we used up the final cylinder last night, before we left.

'Hmm,' our lieutenant says, as the soldier to her other side nudges her and points. We watch as a man – another irregular, as far as I can see – appears from the stable block, puts a drum in the back of one of the four-wheel drives and then starts it, bringing it round to the front of the castle, out of sight from us.

'Much fuel in those cars?' the lieutenant asks quietly.

'Only what we couldn't siphon,' I reply.

'Can you take a vehicle into the castle itself?'

'Not one of those,' I tell her. 'Too tall. There's a small courtyard, with enough room to turn something the size of a jeep around.'

'No drawbridge?' she says, looking at me. I shake my head. She smiles thinly. 'I think you mentioned a gate, though, didn't you, Abel?'

'A thin one, and a portcullis of wrought iron. I doubt either would stop—'

The lieutenant's radio chirps. She holds up one hand to me, and answers the radio, listening then making a snuffing noise. 'Yes, if you can do it cleanly. We're on the ridge just behind the castle.'

She puts the instrument away. 'Amateurs,' she says, sneering, and shakes her head. 'They've nobody in the gatehouse.' She looks at the man to her other side. 'Psycho's in the trees by the drive, over there,' she tells him. 'Says there's only two loading the car. Nothing heavy in sight. He's about to start shooting, then one of the trucks and the other jeep are going to make a dash for the front. Give them cover.' She turns to me. 'These aren't soldiers,' she says with seeming disgust, 'they're just looters.' She shakes her head, then puts the binoculars

24

away and readies her long gun, steadying it and sighting. 'Deathwish,' she says to the soldier with the rocket launcher. 'Save it. Not unless I tell you, okay?'

The fellow looks disappointed.

Gunfire comes from beyond the castle, near where the driveway leaves the trees and climbs up the shallow slope to the main lawn. There is nothing to see for a moment, then the four-wheel drive reappears racing round the gravel track from the front of the castle, back towards the stable block. The car drifts across the gravel, rear door swinging wildly, still open. Its windscreen is starred white and somebody is trying to punch through it from behind. The lieutenant's gun barks suddenly, making me start; the heavy machine-gun they brought from the jeep opens up and I put my hands to my ears. The four-wheel drive shakes, pieces fly off it and it turns sharply, front wheel seeming to buckle, almost tipping it into the moat (the machine-gun's rounds kick tall thin splashes in the water for a moment); the car swerves the other way, losing speed; it straightens out briefly and crashes into the corner of the stable block.

'Stop!' shouts our lieutenant, and the firing ceases.

Steam curls upwards from the car's crushed bonnet. The driver's door opens and somebody falls out, crawling on all-fours on the ground, then collapsing.

Another motor sounds, there is more firing from the front of the castle, and then one of the lieutenant's trucks appears, roaring up the drive, straight for the castle. The gunfire stops; the truck disappears from view, obscured by the castle. We hear its engine rev, then stop altogether.

The rain has ceased. For a few moments there is silence and the only movement comes from the wisps of steam escaping the four-wheel drive's engine. Then we hear a few shouts, and some shots. The lieutenant takes out her radio. 'Mr C?' she says. I hear a crackle in reply.

'Ah, Dopple; what's happening?'

She listens. 'Okay. We got the four-wheel drive; it's out of action. We're coming in now, from the ridge behind. Three minutes.' She puts the radio away. 'Psycho got one at the bridge,' she tells us. 'There's another two or three inside the castle, but the truck got to the gate in time; we're in.' She shoulders her gun. 'Tootight,' she says to the fat soldier I shared the rear of the jeep with. 'You stay here; pop anybody running away who's not one of us.' The fat soldier nods slowly.

Crouched, we move at a half-run between the bushes and trees down to the rear gardens. Isolated shots sound from inside the castle. We go first to the man fallen by the side of the steaming, hissing four-wheel drive. A man lies dead in the passenger seat, his uniform weltered in blood, his jaw half-torn off. The driver lying on the ground is still moaning; blood seeps on to the gravel beneath him. He is a tall, gawky young man with the spotted complexion of adolescence. Our lieutenant squats to slap his face, trying to get some sense from him but extracting only whimpers. Finally she rises, shakes her head, exasperated.

She looks from the wounded man to the soldier with the machine-gun, the one called Karma. He has taken off his steel helmet to wipe his brow; he is red-haired. 'Your turn,' she mutters. 'Come on,' she says to me, as Karma puts his helmet back on, clicks something on the machine-gun and points the weapon at the head of the man lying on the ground. The lieutenant strides off, her boots crunching over the gravel.

I turn quickly and follow her and the soldier with the rocket launcher, a strange tenseness between my shoulder-blades, as though vicariously preparing for the *coup de grâce*. The single, loud bang still makes me jump.

We stand, you and I, in the centre of the castle's courtyard, by the well. We look up and around. The looters have done little damage. The lieutenant quizzed old Arthur – who chose to stay with the castle rather than come with us – and discovered the men arrived only an hour earlier; they barely had time to start sacking our home before our brave lieutenant arrived to the rescue. Now it is hers.

Her men are scrambling everywhere, like children with a new toy. They have a lookout on the battlements, another sentry at the gatehouse; they have mastered the castle's main gate and the portcullis – a recent wrought-iron replacement, perhaps more decorative than effective, but it seems to please them all the same – and are now investigating the cellars, stores and rooms; our servants – surprised, confused – have been told to let them do as they wish; all the doors have been unlocked. The men – though now most of them seem more like boys – are choosing their rooms; it appears they will be our guests for longer than a weekend.

The two jeeps are parked here in the courtyard, the trucks sit outside on the far side of the moat, just over the small stone bridge; our carriage has been returned to the stables, the horses to their paddock. A few of the villagers camping on the lawns, who fled at the approach of the looters, are now returning, warily, to their tents.

The lieutenant appears at the main keep door, sauntering towards us, wearing a new tunic top; a vividly red jacket strung about with bright ropes of gold and studded with medal ribbons. She holds a bottle of our best champagne, already opened.

'There,' she says, looking around at the courtyard walls. 'Not much damage done.' She smiles at you. 'Like my new outfit?' She spins once for us; the red dress jacket swings out.

She fastens a couple of the buttons. 'This was your grandfather's or something?' she asks.

'Some relation; I forget which,' I tell her evenly, as old Arthur, patently the most venerable of our servants, appears at the door with a tray and makes his way slowly towards us.

The lieutenant smiles indulgently at the old man and indicates he should put the tray on the bonnet of one of the jeeps. There are three glasses. 'Thank you . . . Arthur, isn't it?' she says.

The old fellow – rotund, bespectacled, flush-faced, head sparsely yellow-haired – looks uncertain; he nods to the lieutenant, then bows and mutters something to us, before hesitating and walking away. 'Champagne,' the lieutenant says, laughing, already pouring; the ring which she took from you, now encircling her left small finger, clinks against the thick green bulk of the bottle and the long flutes' delicate stems.

We take our glasses. 'To a pleasant stay,' she says, clinking crystal with us. We sip; she gulps.

'Quite how long do you intend to be with us?' I ask.

She says, 'A while. We've been too long on the road, in fields and barns, dossing in half-burnt houses and damp tents. We need some leave from all this soldiering; it gets to you after a while.' She swills her drink around, gazing at it. 'I can see why you left, but we can defend a place like this.'

'We could not,' I agree. 'That's why we chose to leave. May we leave now?'

'You're safer here, now,' she tells us.

I glance at you. 'Still, we would like to leave. May we?'

'No,' the lieutenant says, and sighs. 'I'd like you to stay.'

28

She shrugs, makes to inspect her fine tunic. 'It's my wish.' She adjusts a cuff. 'And rank has its privileges.' Her smile is quite, if briefly, dazzling as she glances about. 'We are your guests, and you are ours. We are willingly your guests; how willing you are ours is up to you.' Another shrug. 'But however that may be, we intend to stay here.'

'And if anyone turns up with a tank, what then?'

She shrugs. 'Then we'd have to leave.' She drinks, and moves the wine around in her mouth for a moment before swallowing. 'But there aren't that many tanks around these days, Abel; there isn't much of anything organised, opposition or otherwise, hereabouts just now. A very fluid situation we have at the moment, after all this mobilisation and waging and prosecuting and attrition and . . .' she waves one hand airily, 'just general breakdown, I suppose.' She puts her head to one side. 'When did you last see a tank, Abel? Or an aircraft, or a helicopter?'

I think for a moment, then just nod to accede.

I sense you looking up. You grab my arm.

The looters; the three our irregulars discovered inside the castle. They surrendered after a few shots and the lieutenant has apparently been questioning them. Now they appear on the roof above, bundled on to the walkway from the tower above the winding-stair by a half-dozen of the lieutenant's soldiers. The three have bags or hoods over their heads and ropes round their necks; they stumble and the way they move makes me think they've been beaten; I can hear what sound like sobs and entreaties from inside the dark hoods. They are being led to the castle's two south-facing towers, whose bases flank the main gate and look over the bridge and moat towards the front lawns and the drive.

Your eyes are wide, your face pale; the gloved hand clutching at me tightens. The lieutenant drinks, watching you closely, something cold and calibratory about her expression. Then, while you still stare at the line of men on the stone skyline, her face animates, becomes relaxed, even cheerful. 'Let's go inside, shall we?' She takes up the tray. 'It's getting cold out here, and it looks like rain.'

Above us, as we troop inside, a young man calls out for his mother.

The lieutenant tethers us in a wing, so that we may fly no more. We dine behind locked doors, on bread and salted meats. In the great hall, our captor entertains her troops with all our roaring kitchens can provide. Predictably, they shot the peacocks. I expected a night of wild debauchery from our new guests, but the lieutenant – according to the whispers of our servants, as they come, escorted, to deliver and remove our meal – has ordered a double guard, no more than one bottle of wine per man, and decreed that our staff and those camping on the lawns be left unmolested. She is wary of attack on this first night, perhaps, and besides her men are weary, with no strength for celebration, only tired relief.

Fires burn in grates, candles flicker before mirrors on many-branched candelabra, and garden torches, unearthed from an outbuilding, burn smokily on walls or stuck in vases, a graceless caricature of medievality.

Meanwhile our looters – their lives negated by a knot, and by that length shortened – swing in the air from towers, stranded in the evening air as a grim signal to the outside world; perhaps the good lieutenant hopes that their swaying will so sway others. To keep them company, the lieutenant and her men have raised a fitting standard on the flagpole; a little joke, they say. It is the skin of a long-dead carnivore they've found;

stalked down some long-neglected corridor, hunted out within a dusty storeroom then finally cornered inside a creaking trunk. And so the old snow-tiger skin flies in the rain-troubled air.

Later, fuelled by their banquet, the lieutenant takes her most trusted men and goes down to those scarred plains we left, to search for what booty, *matériel* or men she can, far into a torchlit night.

CHAPTER
THREE

The castle has a full reserve of memories, their living-on a special sort of death. The lieutenant stalks the night-black plains, the men she left here fall one by one asleep, our servants clean and gather what they can then retire to their quarters, and you, on a chaise with rugs, sleep fitful before a dying logfire. I cannot sleep; instead I pace the three rooms and two short corridors we've been restricted to, carrying a small tricerion to light my way, restless and unsure, and looking from moat to courtyard. On one side there is a moon, half veiled by ragged clouds, shining on the damp sheen of forested hills where mist is gathering. On the other side I see the fitful flicker of a spitting garden torch reflecting on the stone-surrounded cobbles and the well. Even as I watch, that last torch splutters and goes out.

I saw so many dances here. Each ball brought every one of note from counties upon counties away; from each great house, from each plump farm, from over the wooded hills around and across that fertile plain they came, like iron filings to a magnet drawn: sclerotic grandees, rod-backed matrons, amiable buffoons ruddily ho-hoing, indulgent city relations down for a little country air or to kill for sport or find a spouse, beaming boys with faces polished as their shoes, cynical graduates come to sneer and feast, poised observers of the social scene cutting their drinks with their barbed remarks, dough-fresh country youths with invitations clutched, new-blossomed maidens half embarrassed, half proud of their emergent allure; politicians, priests and the brave fighting men; the old money, the new money, the once-monied, the titled and the expleted, the fawn-shy and just the fawning, the well matured and the spoiled . . . the castle had room for all of them.

The great hall resounded like a skull, abuzz with wheeling thoughts, dissimilar and same. The patterns of their music took them, held them, there in its gloved hand, at once fused and confused, and scattered them about the brighter hallways, their laughter like the music for a dream.

The halls and rooms are empty now; the balconies and battlements hang dim, like handholds in the voided dark. In the darkness, in the face of memory, the castle seems now inhuman. Blocked windows mock with the view they no longer afford; here there is a stair's stone spiral disappearing into a blank ceiling where an old tower was levelled, long ago, and here cramped rooms open randomly off one another, implying a passageway, centuries abandoned and reshaped, an appendix within the castle's bowels.

I sit in a tall open window overlooking the moat, watching a rising tide of mist flow up and round to engulf the castle, a great slow wave of star-obscuring darkness upon darkness that unfolds itself from out the forest with a geological inertia and then pushes down upon us.

I recall we danced, those many years ago, and left the ball to see the night, together on those lit battlements that faced the airy dark. The castle was a great stone ship abright and cruising on a sea of black; the plains sparkled with lights, quivering in the intervening air like strings of stars.

We took the air there, you and I, and by and by, took each other's breath, and more exchanged.

'But our parents . . .' you whispered when that first kiss gave way to allow a mutual gasp for air and the incitement to the next. 'But if somebody sees . . .'

Your dress was something black; velvet and pearls if I recall, scooped brocade to its front which, cupping your bosom, gave way beneath my hands. Exposed to the night and my mouth, your breasts were moon-pale and down-smooth, their aureoles and nipples dark as bruises, raised, thick and hard as a little finger's topmost joint; I sucked at you and you leant back, clutching at the stones, drawing the night in sharply through your teeth. Then, in a tiny, unexpected flood, a thick sweet taste came upon my tongue, like a premonition, like some involuntary resonance with the male's expected donation, and in that pallid light two shining beads of your milk shone, one tipping each of those tiny blood-raised towers.

I devoured those pearls, slaking a thirst the more achingly intense for my utter ignorance of it until that moment. You gathered up your gown and skirts yourself, insisted that the winding-stair door be bolted, then I laid you across the slates, beneath the stars.

Was it then I really loved you first? I think it was, my sleeping one. Or perhaps it was later, in a calmer state . . . But I'd count that less; I'd prefer it was just lust. That seems more creditable, simply for being so helpless in the face of its own blood-charged demands.

Love is common; nothing's more so, even hate (even now), and – like their mothers – everyone thinks theirs must be the very best. Oh, the fascination with love, art's profitable fixation with love; ah, the startled clarity, the revelatory force of love, the pulsing certainty that it is all, that it is perfect, that it makes us, that it completes us . . . that it will last for ever.

Ours is a little different, by consent. We became by all accounts – and they were many, and various and frequently creative – notorious; unwilling if unbowed outcasts long before our failed attempt to become refugees. It was our decision, though. Not for us that tawdry fascination, the cosy comfort of the crowd, their bedded warmth in shared exclusion. We see the world with two eyes, tuned for its ambivalence, and what arrests the eye of the small-minded, liberates the mind of those with a broader view. This castle makes its mark upon the earth by being no longer part of the world from which it's raised; these stones inflict themselves upon the air with hard demand that's free to join that higher level only by not joining any rest. We took that as our premise; what else?

I pace these corridors while you sleep by the empty fire (the ashes like a pool, the furs and rugs that cover you the same colour). The clouds roll quietly in around us, damp smoke of what liquidic fire I cannot say. A transient current within the air brings the sound of a distant waterfall from the hills, and only the night finds final voice, in that black space a white noise booming; meaningless.

*   *   *

Morning finds the lieutenant returned to the castle; the mists disperse like a crowd, dew hangs heavy on the forest and the sun, late rising above the southerly hills, shines with a wintery weariness, tentative and provisional as a politician's promise.

The good lieutenant takes her breakfast in our chambers; an old flag – I imagine she does not know it is our family's own arms – has been thrown across the oak table to provide a cloth. She looks tired yet animated, her eyes red and her face flushed. She smells a little of smoke and intends to sleep for a few hours once she has eaten. Her roasted, toasted fare is served on our finest silver; she holds and uses the sharp and glittering pieces of cutlery with a weaponly dexterity. The gold and ruby ring upon her little finger duly sparkles too.

'We found a few things,' the lieutenant replies when I enquire how went the night. 'What we did not find was as important.' She gulps down her milk, sitting back and kicking off her boots. She puts her plate on her lap and her grubbily stockinged feet on the table, selecting and spearing morsels from on high.

'What was it you did not find?' I ask her.

'Many other people,' the lieutenant tells us. 'There were a few refugees, camped out, but nobody . . . threatening; nobody armed, nobody organised.' She picks a few more mouthfuls from her plate of meats and eggs. She gazes ceiling-wards, as if to admire the painted wood panels and embossed heraldic shields. 'We think there may be another group around. Some-where,' she says, then narrows her eyes as she looks at me. 'Competition,' she says, smiling that cold smile of hers. 'Not friends of ours.'

A soft egg-yolk, surgically isolated from its surrounding white and the bed of toast it lay upon by previous incisions, is lifted – intact, yellowly wobbling – on the lieutenant's fork and directed towards her mouth. Her thin lips close around the golden curve. She slips the fork out and holds it vertically, twirling it as her jaw moves and her eyes close. She swallows. 'Hmm,' she says, collecting herself and smacking her lips. 'The last we heard of that happy band they were in the hills, north of here.' She shrugs. 'We couldn't find any sign of them; it may be they've headed east with everybody else.'

'You still intend to remain here?'

'Oh, yes.' She puts the plate down, wipes her lips on a napkin, throws it on the table. 'I like your home very well; I think the boys and I can be happy here.'

'Do you intend to stay long?'

She frowns, takes a deep breath. 'How long,' she asks, 'have your family lived here?'

I hesitate. 'A few hundred years.'

She spreads her arms, 'Well then, what difference can it make if we stay a few days, or weeks, or months?' She digs between two teeth with a ragged fingernail, smiling slyly at you. 'Even years?'

'That depends on how you treat this place,' I say. 'This castle has stood for over four hundred years, but it has been vulnerable to cannon for most of that time and, nowadays, could be destroyed in an hour by a large gun and in a moment with a well-placed bomb or rocket; from inside, all one might need would be a match in the right place. The effects of our tenure here as a family unfortunately has no bearing on yours as occupiers, especially given the circumstances prevailing outside these walls.'

The lieutenant nods wisely. 'You're right, Abel,' she says, rubbing one index finger beneath her nose and staring at her smudge-grey socks. 'We are here as occupiers, not your guests, and you are our prisoners, not our hosts. And this place suits our purposes; it's comfortable, defendable, but it means no more to us.' She picks up her fork again, inspects it minutely. 'But these men aren't vandals. I've told them not to break anything and if they do it will assuredly be clumsiness rather than insubordination. Oh, there are a few extra bullet-holes about the place, but most of any damage you might see was probably caused by your looters.' She wipes something from the tines of the fork, then licks her fingers. 'And we made them pay quite dearly for such ... despicable desecration.' She smiles at me.

I glance at you, my dear, but your eyes are averted now, your gaze cast down. 'And us?' I ask our lieutenant. 'How do you intend to treat us?'

'You – and your wife?' she says, then watches keenly. I display, I hope, no reaction. You look away, towards the window. 'Oh, with respect,' the lieutenant continues, nodding, expression serious. 'Why, with honour.'

'But not to the extent of honouring our desire to leave.'

'Correct!' she says. 'You're my local knowledge, Abel. You know your way around these parts.' She gestures upwards and around. 'And I've always had a thing about castles; you can give me a guided tour of the place, if you like. Well, let's be honest; if I like. And I do like. You wouldn't mind, though, would you, Abel? No, of course not. I'm sure it would be a treat for you as well. I'm sure you have lots of interesting stories you can tell me about the place; fascinating ancestors, famous visitors, exciting incidents, exotic heirlooms from faraway lands ... Ha! For all I know the place even has a ghost!' She sits forward, the fork waved in her fingers like a wand. 'Does it, Abel? Does the place have a ghost?'

I sit back. 'Not yet.'

This makes her laugh. 'There you are. Your real treasures are things the looters weren't interested in; the place itself, its history, the library, the tapestries, ancient chests, old clothes, statues, great gloomy paintings . . . all still intact, pretty much. Perhaps while we're here you can educate my men; give them a taste for culture. I'm sure my own aesthetic senses have been heightened already, just talking to you and sitting here.' She clatters the fork down on the salver. 'That's the thing, you see; people like me get so few opportunities to talk to people like you and stay in places like this.'

I nod slowly. 'Yes, and you know who I am, who we are; there are books in the library listing the generations of our family, and portraits of most of our ancestors on every wall, but we don't know who you are. Might we inquire?' I glance at you; your gaze has returned to the lieutenant. 'Just a name would do,' I tell her.

She scrapes her seat back, flexing her shoulders, arching her back and stifling the greater part of a yawn. 'Of course,' she says, linking her hands and stretching them against each other. 'What you don't realise, until you become part of one, is the way that units in the front line – the grunts, the squaddies – take on nicknames. They leave their civilian names behind with their civilised personalities; they become another person, after training. Maybe it's a sort of shamanistic thing, like a lucky charm.' She grins. 'You know; the bullet with your name on it will have your non-com handle printed thereon, not the real one, the one your buddies call you.' She snorts. 'You know I've forgotten the real name of every man in this squad? Been with some of them two years, too, and that seems like a very long time, in the circumstances?' She nods. 'But, their names . . . Well, there's Mr Cuts—'

'He alive?' I suggest.

She looks at me oddly, then continues. 'He's kind of my deputy; a sergeant in his old unit. Then there's Airlock,

Deathwish, Victim, Karma, Tootight, Kneecap, Verbal, Ghost
– Ah!' she smiles suddenly. 'See; we have a ghost already!'
She sits forward, flicking the names off, finger by finger.
'. . .Ghost, Lovegod, Fender, Dropzone, Grunt, Broadleaf,
Poppy, One-track, Dopple, Psycho . . . and . . . that's all,'
she says, sitting back, closing up, crossing her arms and legs.
'There was Half-caste, but he's dead now.'

'Was he the young man on the road yesterday?'

'Yes,' she says quickly. Then is silent for a moment. 'You
know the strange thing?' She looks at me. I watch. 'I remem-
bered Half-caste's name, his old name, civilian name, when
I kissed him.' Another moment's pause. 'It was . . . Well, it
doesn't matter now.'

'Then you killed him.'

She looks at me for a long time. I have out-stared many a
man, but those cold grey globes come close to besting me.
Eventually, she says, 'Do you believe in God, Abel?'

'No.'

What must be one of the lieutenant's smallest-calibre smiles
is dispatched. 'Then just wish that you aren't ever dying from
a stomach wound when there's nobody around armed with
anything better than a skin plaster and the sort of painkillers
you'd use for a mild hangover. And nobody prepared to put
you out of your agony.'

'You have no medic?'

'Had. Got in the way of some mortar shrapnel two weeks
ago. Name was Vet,' she says, yawning again. 'Vet,' she
repeats, and puts her arms behind her head, as though in surrender (her gaudy jacket falls open and, within her army shirt,
the lieutenant's breasts press briefly out; I suspect they might
be, like her, quite firm). 'Not because he was long-serving. Still,
you take what you can get, you know?'

43

'So, at the end of this, what ought we to call you?' I ask, thinking to break her out of such dreadful sentimentality.

'You really want to know?'

I nod.

'Loot,' she tells me, passing bashful. Another shrug. 'After a while, you become your function, Abel. I am the lieutenant, so they call me Loot. I have become Loot. It is what I answer to.'

'Lute, with a U?'

She smiles. 'No.'

'And before that?'

'Before?'

'What were you called before?'

She shakes her head, snorts. 'Easy.'

'Easy?'

'Yes. I used to say, "Easy, now," a lot. It got shortened.' She inspects her nails. 'I'll thank you not to use it.'

'Indeed; the jibes that suggest themselves would be . . . eponymous.'

She regards me, narrow-eyed for a moment, then says, 'Just so.' She yawns, then rises. 'And now I'm going to sleep,' she announces, stretching her arms. She stoops to gather up her boots. 'I thought we might – the three of us – take a walk, later on; into the hills,' she says. 'Maybe do some hunting, this afternoon.' She passes me by and pats me on the shoulder. 'You two make yourselves at home.'

CHAPTER
FOUR

I regret I am impressed with our lieutenant, if mildly. She has a sort of uncut grace, and I find her lack of beauty (as she does, not unthinking) beyond the point. I do not like people who make me notice what they fail to find impressive in themselves.

You rise and walk round the table, straightening the flag as you approach, then stand behind me, hands on my shoulders, gently pressing, kneading, massaging. I let you work my tired muscles for a while, my body rocking slightly, my head moving slowly back and forth. I do believe sleep may be coming at last; my eyes half close, and a sleepy focus brings my gaze to the surface of our flag, spread upon the table. Dried mud

47

lies scattered on the flag, a souvenir of the plains delivered courtesy of the lieutenant's boots. No doubt their soil lies sprinkled over most of our rooms, corridors and rugs by now. My gaze, filtered through the blurring eyelash veil of my half-closed eyes, stays fixed upon that caked dirt lying on our colours, and I recall our second tryst.

I threw you on this same flag once, though not on this table, not in this room. Somewhere higher than here; an old attic, dusty and warm with the day's soaked-in sunlight. On the other side of those slates we had used as a prop to our pleasure the night before, we crept while the rest of our party, still recovering from the night's excitement, lunched on the lawns or soaked away hangovers in baths. I wanted you immediately – my desire stoked but smothered, banked for the rest of that night first by your too proper concern for our absence being noticed, then by the sleeping arrangements, which meant we each had to share a room with other relations – but you demurred at first, in some recollected aftermath of shyness.

And so, like the children we no longer were, we investigated old boxes, trunks and chests, our declared pretext become real. We found old clothes, moth-eaten fabrics, ancient uniforms, rusted weapons, empty boxes, whole crates of hard, heavy phonograph records, forgotten urns, vases and bowls and a hundred other discarded pieces of our history, recent and antique, risen here like light detritus upon the swirling currents of the castle's fluid vitality, deposited at its dusty, unused summit like dusty memories in an old man's head.

We tried on some old clothes; I brandished an age-spotted sword. The flag, unfolded from a trunk, made a carpet for our shoes and discarded clothes, then – after I grew bolder, taking off more, helping you with your assumed attire, letting my hands and fingers linger, then kissing – it became our bed.

Within the arid calm of that dark, abandoned place, our passion took and shook the flag, rumpling and creasing it as though to a slow storm it had been exposed, until I dampened it with a sparse rain more precious than air and storm-clouds ever have to offer.

I recalled those offered moon-pearls of the night before, and on the flag it was as though they now lay returned, *memento vivae* unstrung upon a sewn-on and now crumpled shield, with swords and some mythic beast shown rampant.

You drained me, sequentially; our pleasure became pain and I discovered that you suffered in silence, and screamed – quiet, hoarse, bitten off – for satisfaction only. We fell asleep eventually in each other's arms, and on our family's.

You took your repose like your pleasure, sleeping one eye half-open, above an embroidered, fading unicorn. We slept an hour away, then dressed and – luckily unseen – hurried down apart; you to a bath and I to a hillside walk we each pretended had begun long before.

You continue, working my shoulders, stroking my neck, pressing into the top of my back. My gaze remains fixed upon the mud the lieutenant's boots have left. When I was young, just a child – and you were away, held from me by that family dispute our mating somehow sought to mend – I remember that for my early years I hated dirt and mud and grime more than anything else I could imagine. I'd wash my hands after every contact with something I thought unclean, running in even from sports and games outside to rinse off under the nearest tap what was no more than honest earth, as though terrified that somehow I might be contaminated by that mundanity.

I blame, of course, my mother, an essentially urban woman; that excess of fastidiousness which she encouraged served me ill for those young years, bringing down upon my head a shower of insults from my friends, peers and relations more filthy than anything I thought I might pick up from wood, ground or park.

It was a horror of the common; something Mother thought was ingrained, indeed genetic, within both our class and particularly our family, but insufficiently so by her strict standards; something which required reinforcement, feeding, bringing on and bringing up, like a carefully trained flower or a well-bred and well-groomed horse.

My fanatical cleanliness was the symbol of my worship of my mother, and the acknowledgement, the very expression of our superiority compared to those beneath us. It was a belief which Mother was perfectly appalled she could not effectively evangelise to others of our station. I knew of people of our kind – as well connected, as ancient in their lineage, as abundant in the extent of their estates – who, as far as my mother was concerned, entirely let down the side by living as meanly – or at least as grubbily – as any peasant with bare feet, an earth floor and a single change of clothes. I knew people who owned half a county who habitually packed more dirt beneath their fingernails than my mother considered decent in a window box, whose breath and person smelled so that it was possible to detect their earlier presence in a room for half a day subsequently and who, save for the most special of occasions, dressed in old clothes so tatty, torn and holed that each new servant brought into their employ had to be carefully instructed, should they come into contact with these rags on the rare circumstance when they were not being worn by their owner, not to pick them up between finger and thumb and at arm's length take them promptly to the nearest fire or outside bin.

Mother regarded such laxity with disgust; of course it was easy to live as one wanted when there was no one to tell you otherwise and one possessed an income independent of external sanitary sanction, but that was precisely the point; the poor had an excuse for their grubbiness while the better-off had none, and to reveal oneself as being happy to live in conditions which might unnerve a pig was an insult both to those like my mother who clove to the true faith of immaculate hygiene, and indeed to those less fortunate as well.

My thoughts on such matters matched those of Mother perfectly; they were the very image of hers, and I remained her disciplined disciple in all this until one day in early spring, at the age of nine, when I was walking alone in the woods to the north of the castle. I had had an argument with my tutor and my mother and, when my lessons had concluded for the day, had stormed from the house, not noticing the rain that was approaching from the west. The wind surprised me underneath the still bare trees, a loud commotion shaking their tops, and only then did I turn back towards the castle, clutching my thin coat around me, seeking in the pockets for gloves that were not there.

Then the rain came, plunging in a cold fusillade through the near-naked branches of the broad-leaved trees where only the first hints of bright buds broke the brown monotony of bark. I cursed Mother, and my tutor. I cursed myself, for paying too little heed to the weather and for neglecting to ensure I had both cap and gloves with me. The coat – my best, another foolishness born of angry haste – snagged on branches as I made my way back down. My shoes, polished to a gleam, already bore scuffs and were spattered with dirt. I cursed the grasping trees, the whole noisome forest, the dung-shaped hills themselves and the dark, spitting weather (though only, it must be said, in terms that would have made Mother frown a little – I believed as did Mother that my mouth as much as my well-scrubbed skin must stay unsoiled).

The path angled down the side of a hill, beneath the tall, swaying trunks; it zigged and zagged, taking a shallow, easy route towards the castle, but long. The rain, by now tumultuous, stung my cheek, plastered my hair to my head and started to insinuate its way down the back of my neck, icily intimate and crawling like a cold centipede against my skin. I roared at the heedless hills, the witless weather and my own cursed luck. I stopped by the side of the track, looked down and determined to cut out the bends in the path and head straight down the slope.

I skidded twice on a slurry of mud and decaying leaves, and had to clutch at the wet and slimy ground to prevent myself from falling further. Cold muck and the rotted humus of the previous year's fall squelched between my fingers, gelid, brown and troughed; I wiped my hands on the grass as best I could, leaving smears. My treasured coat was growing heavy with the rain, its surface everywhere darkened by the incessant drops, its cut elegance made loose and incontinent by the lathering rain, probably ruining it for ever.

At the bottom of the route I'd chosen there was a steep bank and a deep ditch to negotiate before I could regain the path; I blinked through the water streaming down my face, looking this way and that, trying to see an easier passage, but the bank and ditch ran on to each side and there was no simpler route. I decided to jump, but even as I stepped back to gather myself for the leap, the bank gave way beneath me, sending me tumbling and flailing down the muddy slope. I collided with exposed roots and was thrown outwards, landing on my back on the far side of the ditch, knocking all the wind out of me and smacking my head back on a stone, and then – winded, dizzy, helplessly disoriented – I could not help myself rebounding, falling forward, into the dark soiled depths of the ditch.

I lay there, hands clawed into the filth on either side, my face stuck into the rank mud. I pulled my head free of the earth's cloying grip, eructing the muck from out my nose and mouth, gagging as I spat and snorted out its thick, cold mucus. I tried to breathe, swallowing between spits and splutters and attempting to force my lungs to work while a terrible vacuum I could not fill sat within my chest, mocking me.

I rolled over, still wheezing for my breath, thinking in a panic that I might die here, suffocating in the midst of these woods' frigid excrement; perhaps I had broken something; perhaps this awful sucking inability to take a breath was the onset of a terrible, spreading paralysis.

The rain plummeted down at me. It cleaned my face a little, but my neck and back were sinking down into the mud and my shoes were filled with cold, filthy water. Still I laboured for air. I started to see strange lights above me in the trees, even as the totality of the view dimmed, and the air roared at me like an obscene lullaby presaging death.

I forced myself to sit up, kneel, then get on all-fours to cough and hack once more, and finally persuaded some spittle-charged air to whistle down my throat towards my lungs. I gagged and spluttered again and stared down at the brown glue of mulch and soil flowing up around my hands; it rose until the dark tide quite covered them and only my wrists showed, pale against the muddy swirl, while below the scummy surface my hands kneaded the giving, pliant, warming mud that suddenly felt like flesh.

I coughed once more and sneezed, and watched long glutinous strings loop down from my mouth and nose, attaching
me to the soil until, with one enmired hand, I brushed them
away.

I began to breathe more easily at last, then, believing that I
would not now die and had not been seriously injured, I looked
about me. I gazed at the lashing drops sprinkling all around,
at the slick, swollen curve of the ditch's flank, bordered by a
soaking skirt of heavy, drooping grass, at the darkly towering
trees standing imperiously over me, at the thin, gauzy veils of
rain still sweeping and drifting through the moistened forest, at
the little silky rivulets of water running down over glistening,
limb-like roots protruding from the earthy bank and flowing
across the surface of the path like some rough, chill sweat of
the land.

Somehow, I began to laugh. I coughed once more as I did
so, but still; I laughed and wept and shook my head and
then flopped forward into the dun sludge, surrendering to
it, making swimming motions within its glutinous embrace
as I tried to gather it to me, squeezing it between my fingers,
taking it into my mouth, smearing it on to my face, drinking
it. I started to strip off my soaking clothes, wriggling wetly
from them, casting them aside, half maddened, half incited by
their cloying, clinging resistance, until finally I was naked in
the cold filth, rolling in it like a dog in ordure, freezing and
numb but laughing and growling, smoothing that slime all over
my body, excited by its clammy caress so that the cold and wet
fought a losing battle with my own raised heat, and in a while
I knelt there in the bottom of the ditch, plastered in streaked
mud and – for the first time in my life – masturbating.

There was no issue, the soil went unsoiled and I did not
truly join the earth then, but after that dry and fiery coming,

and with that warm, thigh-deep glow still echoing within me, I dressed, shivering, and cursed the grainily slick, damply uncooperative clothes. My curses were more florid now; I used language appropriated from some gardeners I'd overheard months before, those cuttings only now taking root within my soul and blooming from a now quite thoroughly fouled mouth.

The rain was clearing by the time I returned to the castle; I accepted the servants' attentions, Mother's kindly shrieks and busy sympathy and gladly took the warm, steaming bath, the fluffed towels, the clouding, perfumed talc and the sweet cologne, then let myself be dressed in crisp, clean clothes, but there was something else I wore now, something that was now part of myself, like the gritty water I had swallowed in the ditch and which was slowly making its way through my system, becoming, in part, part of me.

Mud, dirt, filth, soil, the very earth itself, in all its slimy, scatological uncouthness, could be a source of pleasure. There was an ecstasy in letting go, a value in continence beyond its own reward. To remain aloof, to stay unsullied, to maintain a certain distance from the unholy marl of life could make the final embracing, the eventual taking and possessing of that fundamental quality, one of one's most sweetly precious, even blissfully acute pleasures.

I think Mother looked upon me differently from that day on. I know I regarded myself as being someone quite distinct from the boy who had set out upon that walk. I tried to remain as civil and polite as Mother might desire when I was in her company or with those on whom she knew she could rely, through good or bad reports, to provide a vicarious presence, but in my soul I was a new and knowledgeable creature, possessed of a certain wisdom, and no longer really hers.

No more advice, no censure, rules nor even love itself could she offer me in the future, without it being measured against the intelligence of that taste for base surrender and brazen possession I had discovered in myself, inside the saturating force of that deluge, descent and fall.

CHAPTER
FIVE

I n the afternoon we go hunting. The lieutenant's men mostly
nurse their wounds or sleep; a few scout close at hand. Our
servants have begun to clean the castle, dusting beneath
the odd bullet-hole, tidying up after the soldiers, sorting and
washing and drying. Only the trio of dangling looters are
denied their attentions; the lieutenant wants them to stay
where they are, as a warning and a reminder. Meanwhile
the camp of displaced persons outside on our lawns has filled
up once again; people from burned farms and villages shelter
amongst our gazebos and pavilions, set up tents on the croquet
lawn and draw water from the ornamental ponds; our trout
suffer the same fate as the peacocks did last night. A few

more fires burn outside the tents and makeshift shelters, and suddenly, in the midst of our gentle estate, we have a *barrio*, a *favela*, our own little township. The soldiers have already searched the camp; for weapons, they said, but found only what they decided was an inexcusable excess of food and a few more bottles of drink that could not to be allowed to fall into the wrong throats.

The day is almost warm as we tramp into the hills beneath calm, slow-moving clouds. The lieutenant has me lead the way; she follows with you. Bringing up the rear are two of her men, carrying their own rifles and a canvas bag heavy with shotguns.

The lieutenant chatters on, pointing out species of trees, bushes and birds, talking of hunting as though she knows much about it, constructing impressions of how you and I must have lived in more peaceful times. You listen; I do not look back, but I imagine I can hear you nod. The path is steep; it leads up through the trees and over the ridge behind, then mostly follows the course of the stream which feeds the castle grounds and moat, crossing and recrossing it on small wooden bridges through steep gullies and dark clefts of broken rock where the water roars luminous and rushing beneath and the sky is a bright mirror above, cracked and crazed by the bare limbs of the trees. The mud and leaf-mulch makes the footing uncertain, and a few times I hear you slip, but the lieutenant catches you, holds you, helps you up and on, laughing and joking all the while.

Higher up, I take us out of our own woods and into a neighbour's; if this farce must take place at least it will not do so on what were our lands.

The lieutenant makes much show of letting us both have guns; she places one in your arms, hands another to me. I have to break it to make sure it is not already loaded. The two soldiers she had carry the weapons stand back, their own rifles ready – safety catches off, I note. The lieutenant will reload her single gun – she was disappointed we had no pump-action devices – but we are in the privileged position of having a brace each; the soldiers will reload for us.

Upon a high crest of moor, the lieutenant stands statuesque, field-glasses raised, surveying the plains, river, road and distant castle, seeking out her prey. 'There,' she says. She hands the binoculars to you. 'Can you see the castle? See the flag?'

Your gaze flies across the view and comes to rest; you nod slowly. You wear a hunting jacket, dark culottes, a practical hat and boots; the lieutenant mostly sports her camouflaged combat gear, but with a stalker's hat. I thought to dress in a suit more suited to an afternoon's informal reception than a hike and hunt in the hills, but this light touch does not seem to have registered with our good lieutenant. In this raised place, our full absurdity seems bared; we take such pains looking for dumb little things to kill, when all about – upon the plain, within the lower hills, in distant towns and cities, in every place where the maps show human habitation – lies evidence of atrocity and a self-provided surfeit of blood-slicked slaughterers; fitter targets, I'd have thought, requiring no excuse, no manufactured, cultured analogue of ire to make them quarry.

'Shh!' our lieutenant says, tipping her head just so. We all listen, and there, upon the turning wind, borne hush-hushing across the trees' high heads, we hear the gut-grumble, the half-earthfelt thuds of distant artillery.

'You hear that?' she asks.

You nod. As does she, thoughtfully. The slow beat falls across us; a pair of clapping, huge-made hands, hollow earth and sonorous air booming together. The lieutenant takes the field-glasses from you and with those cold grey eyes interrogates the lands exposed below, sweeping over them, turning and returning, searching in vain for the source of the ghostly bombardment.

'Over the hills and far away,' she says softly. Finally the noise fades, hauled away on some unseen surface within the wind. She shrugs and returns to her original intent in these inclines, fixes upon an edge of deep forest some way along the hillside and bids us all head in that direction. Soon we are standing before the plantation; a wall of dark green across the swelling slope.

I cannot imagine we will find anything to shoot here; I tried to be as noncommittal as possible, earlier, while the lieutenant was planning this escapade. I had been vague concerning what there was to shoot and where, claiming that I'd required the services of a faithful retainer long departed to show me where to stand and point my gun, though I did hazard that this might not be the right time of year for what she seemed to have in mind. Perhaps she would prefer deer, or boar, or sheep?

Still, coming to a fold in the hills where the forest makes a shallow V, we come upon a pool and a whole flock of little sipping birds; some type of finch, I believe. The lieutenant urges us to be ready, checks that her men are watching us and not our prey, then looses the first discharges while the creatures are still too far away and on the ground. The birds lift and wheel, scattering then bunching as the flock rushes into the sky. The lieutenant whoops and hurdles a fence, reloading on the run. You and I look at each other. Our escorts, too, exchange glances, unsure what to do. The birds circle, flying over us as the lieutenant, now underneath them, fires again. You raise your gun and fire. I do not. A couple of feather-puffs in the air and two down-spiralling bodies betoken some success.

'Come on!' the lieutenant shouts, arm windmilling. Her beaters come forward; one prods me in the back with his rifle. We advance, while the flock beats off down-slope, away; the lieutenant fires once more and another tiny, jerking body drops to the tufted grass. The low baseline of distantly thundering field-pieces begins again, as the lieutenant spots some squirrels scooting up a nearby tree; she lets rip against these tiny targets and ends their comic scampering in a small explosion of twig, leaf, needle, fur and blood. We join her at the margin of a mixed stand of trees as she kicks through some thorn bushes and reloads again; her face is flushed, her breathing quick.

'Verbal, pick up the birds we get, will you?' One of the soldiers trudges off to retrieve the trophies the lieutenant has gathered so far. 'How do you—?' she begins, then goes quiet and raises one hand. 'Verbal, down!' she hisses. The soldier picking up the dead birds drops, obedient as any hound. Another flock of birds is circling, curving down-slope from a pass in the mountains; it wheels and dips above the pond, a single entity of brown-black whirring dots like a swarm contained within a huge invisible bag, elastic sided, rushing over the trees, down to the pool, back up and then back down, expanding and reshaping, cleaving and then cleaving and then, with a final rush, settling. The lieutenant glances at us, nods, then fires.

Lead shot bursts amongst the waters of the pool, a thousand little splashes amongst the panicking flock's desperate flutterings.

The lieutenant glances at me, briefly frowning then smiling. 'Bad form, eh, Abel?' she shouts. She breaks the gun, and cartridges pop smoking out. 'But good fun!' she concludes, and laughs. I wait until the birds are in the air, then fire to miss, too low. You bag another one or two. The lieutenant, still laughing, has time to reload once more before the flock can fully escape; her targets fly up over us, above the trees, and her shots bring down a hail of leaves and twigs pattering through themselves. In amongst them the dying birds fall too; a petty debris-death, committed within the echoes and re-echoes – though I think the lieutenant does not hear them – of the greater conflict in the lower world.

An excited wait, hiding in the edge of the woods, then another flight of birds appears. I start to wonder if this is the same idiot bunch coming back each time, memories too short to remember their recent losses, but this flock is larger than the groups we've seen so far and I think the lieutenant has stumbled upon the migratory route for this species as they come southwards for the winter through the high valleys.

The lieutenant stands, fires, advances and fires again, blasting birds out of the air; you bring down another before the flock disperses. I leave my gun broken across my arm; no one seems to notice.

The lieutenant's men take the tiny bodies and stuff them in old cartridge sacks. You excuse yourself, stalking off into the dark forest behind. The lieutenant, breathless from her fun, smiles after you, then looks to me.

'Take part, Abel,' she says with a tight smile, glancing at my gun. 'Mustn't be dead weight on this sort of outing, must we?'

'You seemed to be doing so well,' I tell her, disingenuous. 'I felt positively peripheral.'

Her lips purse briefly. 'I'm sure. But it looks bad, doesn't it? One has to make an effort.'

'Does one?'

She glances after you again. 'Morgan's doing her best; she seems to be enjoying herself, as far as I can tell.' She frowns.

'She is of an amenable nature.'

'Hmm,' the lieutenant says, nodding, still looking after you. 'She's very quiet, isn't she?'

'That is just her thinking aloud,' I tell the lieutenant, with a gracious smile.

I do believe she seems taken aback. Then she laughs lightly. 'My, sir,' she says softly, 'you are harsh.'

I look towards where you have disappeared in the sea-dim depths of the tall tree-trunks. 'Some people appreciate a little harshness,' I tell her.

She thinks about this, then takes a deep breath. 'Really? A taste for harshness?' She looks up to the sky and scans about. 'What a lot of contented people there must be around then, these days.'

She breaks her gun, ejecting the cartridges, carefully emplaces another pair. 'So,' she says, flicking the gun closed one-handed. I wince. 'Are you two married? Is she your wife?'

'Not as such.'

Still one-handed, she sights down the barrels at the ground. 'But in effect.'

'Quite. In fact, a closer relationship than most.'

I think the lieutenant wanted to inquire further, but at that moment you return, smiling shyly, gaze cast down, and take up your gun again. Above, another smaller flock rounds in, all unsuspecting.

We shoot some more. I aim to fail again, you have some success but never were a good gun, while the lieutenant seems to have discovered a gift, scattering dead and dying birds all about the fringes of the pool.

'You seem a poor shot, Abel,' she tells me, stern-faced, while her men retrieve her haul. 'I assumed you'd be much better.' She brandishes her shotgun. 'Were all these guns for others? Don't you shoot at all?'

'I'm used to larger targets,' I say, truthfully enough.

'So's Lovegod.' She grins at one of the soldiers. 'Let him have a shot.'

I have to surrender my gun. The soldier – a stiff, awkward-looking youth with a face a decade older than his frame – requires a little instruction, but then quite takes to the sport. His comrade continues to reload your gun. The cartridge sack of feathered corpses is shoved into my hands and I am reduced to the gathering after their hunting.

'Good, Lovegod!' the lieutenant tells her charge as we wait between waves of birds. 'Lovegod's doing very well, don't you think, Morgan?' You give a small smile which may be assent. 'Pretty good for a wounded man. Show her your scars, Lovegod.'

The young soldier looks hesitant as he bares his shoulder – happily not the one taking a hammering from the shotgun – and shows you some grubby bandages. 'And the rest; don't be shy!' the lieutenant growls, half-scornful, slapping the fellow on his behind.

The young man has to undo his trousers, dropping them to his knees as his face flushes. Another thick bandage round one upper thigh (I had not even noticed he limped, though now I think about it, he did). His pants look even greyer than his bandages, and his face now darker still than both. I begin to feel sorry for the lad.

'Close one there, eh, Lovegod?' the lieutenant says, winking. The youth gives a nervous laugh and quickly does himself up again. You have looked away. 'Lovegod had a narrow escape,' the lieutenant tells you, scanning the sky for more sport. 'Shrapnel, wasn't it, Lovegod?' The soldier boy grunts, still embarrassed. 'Shell,' the lieutenant informs us. 'Could even have been fired by one of the guns we can hear now,' she says, eyes narrowing, nose raised to the wind. The two soldiers look puzzled and you give no sign. I concentrate, and there indeed, now I'm listening for it again, is that distant, nearly subsonic rumble of the faraway artillery. 'Ah . . .' the lieutenant breathes, as another blur of tiny birds rush down from the higher slopes and circle in the air round the pool.

Several of the birds, only wounded, fall one-wing fluttering, trapped in a tiny confusion of fallen, blasted leaves to land near your feet, hitting the ground to cheep and flap about with eccentric self-concern, only to be stood on.

When you were younger, you would have cried to hear their tiny skulls crack so. But you have learned to look away and inspect your gun, or with those strands of spent smoke greyly curling against your worn-up hair, break it and reload.

Ah, did I desire you at that moment; I wanted you for that night, unwashed, half dressed, in a tangle of clothes and rugs and boots and belts, anxious by an eager, open fire while that cartridge powder perfume lingered blackly on your skin and in your let-down hair.

It was not to be. Having granted me the status of hound for the rest of our shoot and filling two sacks with the booty, the lieutenant orders me to an early bed like a fractious child, on our return to the castle.

It was, I think, for my transgression. Between gun-dog and child, I become briefly a pack animal, ordered to carry the heavy, warm sacks of dead birds and a broken gun on our way back home by the same steep route.

Behind me, the lieutenant talks on, regaling you with her life; another broken home. A mean start in less troubled times, modest victories at school and sport building a dawning self-esteem and leading to a slow and self-determined struggle up from the rest of the herd. There followed a stint at some college then – with the coy hint of a disappointment in love – the decision to enlist, some time before the onset of the present hostilities.

Tiresomely, then, one of those for whom such troubles are in truth a liberation, providing the making of the individual character within the theatre of this greater destruction; a contrarily minor eddy of creation in these fiercely corrosive times. Our lieutenant's is a spirit freed by the re-ordering implicit in this general disorder; a beneficiary, so far, of the conflict. That which has dragged us down has buoyed her up, and, in the castle, we meet, mirrored, and perhaps pass.

I might like to hear more of our captor's story, but seeing my opportunity I drop my precious cargo. On the first bridge across the stream I slip and clutch at the damply greasy rail, letting the bulky sacks drop from me, with the gun, so all the lieutenant's catch goes flying down to the rapids far below. The gun just disappears without a fuss, its own splash lost within the endless foaming rush of that steep stream. The sacks fall more slowly, hit a swirling pool and let forth their dead. The birds sail out, the foaming water fills with feather, lead and flesh, and the wet birds – water-skinnied even further – float and circle and peel off and race away in that airy torrent.

I rise slowly, wiping green slime from my hands. The lieutenant comes up to me, grim-faced. She glances over the side of the bridge at the noisy, eddying surge below, as all her booty speeds away. 'That was careless, Abel,' she tells me through lips like a grey-pink wound and teeth which seem disinclined to part.

'Perhaps I chose the wrong shoes,' I offer, apologetic. She

looks down at my brown brogues; reasonably rustic in aspect but with poor soles for such terrain.

'Perhaps,' she says. I do believe I am frightened of her, just for this moment. I could believe that she is capable of blowing a hole in me with her shotgun, or putting a bullet from her pistol through my head, or even just having me thrown over this wooden parapet by her men. Instead she takes one last glance at where the birds have disappeared within the rocky race and, in that cataract losing sight of them, has the soldiers load me with the remaining guns. 'I really wouldn't lose those, Abel,' she says, sounding almost sad. 'Really.' She turns away. 'Watch our friend carefully,' she tells the man behind me. 'We don't want him slipping again. That would be too terrible. Eh, my lady?' she asks as she passes you. We tramp on, and leave the river's roar buried in its chasm.

I am closed within a high and unused room, a silted backwater in the east tower's highest floor. Cluttered, it is, jumbled with all the froth of our living, like our fond-remembered attic. The small windows are mostly smashed, their sills spattered with bird droppings. The fractured panes let in chill rain; I stuff some old curtains into the spaces. In the cold grate I light a fitful fire from bound, collected volumes of old and yellow-paged magazines, some of them dealing with hunting and other rural matters; it seems appropriate.

This theme continues. I cannot believe the good lieutenant memorised the castle's every room on one tour round, so I conclude it is just luck that she has me confined here, with these old journal collections, and – in glass cases – trophies of previous hunts. Animals, birds and fish stare out, glassy eyed and stiffly posed, like awkward ancestors in paintings. The cases are locked; I look for keys in vain, so force a few of these glass sarcophagi, splintering the wood and fracturing the glass.

Regarding the stuffed fowl, the gutted fish, the glass-eyed fox and hare, I tap their hard, dead eyes, sniff their dustless plumage and stroke their strange dry skins. Feathers and scales stay with my hand. I hold them up to the candelight, trying to see their link, the time-slow change from sea to air, from scale to feather, tail to tail, iridescence to iridescence that these ends unravel back to, expressing evolution's glacial, erratic continuity. The scale, so small, stays too great, however, and remains unseen.

I throw open a narrow window over the moat and launch the birds; they fall. I heave the fish out to the waters; they float. I suppose this is the extra element revealed; the quickness found in living things which ranks above the rest and makes fire, air, earth and water seem closer to each other than ever they are to it.

Just so, the bird and fish, elementally distinguished, are more similar to each other than either is to us. (I stretch the unpinned wings – they grate upon their keel. The lithe trout's body, a single fluid muscle wrapped in rainbow tissue, stays inflexible as bone.) But theirs is a beauty of extremity, and I remember catching sight of a bat, silhouetted against a floodlight, its skin like translucent paper, each long and tiny bone picked out in a tracery of exposed flight; the thing was comely but the outline of elongated limb, the paw-shape stretched out contorted to become half the wing itself, looked like some preposterous distortion, a mad exaggeration of form which nature somehow ought to feel guilty for. The grace and poise bestowed upon the beast by that exaggerated reformation of its inherited parts, from hand to wing, is something that hands alone, need time and a mind to fashion so decidingly.

70

I throw the useless things away, burning them on the bed of pages. Before I go to bed, on a platform of boxes, rugs and cloaks, I eat the tray of roasted peahen, plucked but dressed, you have the lieutenant send to me.

I dreamt that night, and in amongst the amber wreckage of your eyes, like a fractured glass containing your chill spirit, hazy visions of a brighter fate swam slow. It was, in the end, the usual thing, the ordinary speciality of our minds' house, a seamy buffeting wrestled out within the pillowed folds of the brain; desire expressed, wishing to impress. Yet, like an old book by fire or dampness warped, around the edges of this fancy lurked my submerged thought (or dream's the fire, consuming, the mind the centre, the little bit unburned, the prose reduced, promoted to a random poesy).

And I have written you, my dear; I have left my mark, my pen's spilled, I've left you soiled and more than my tongue has lashed, falling, to raise the scores. Cut, hurt, tied, taken, left, you want what you do not want and get it; a kinder fate, it suits me to consider, than really wanting what you do, and not.

But by being less than tender on occasion, I have made you rare, and what we share is not much shared. I have watched servants, farmhands, mechanics and secretaries make that backward beast, I have observed their palled equality with our own state, and been with that cosy ordinariness, that unthinkingly smug normality, perversely disgusted.

I have decided, however coldly, that for any of this life, this passing thought of mind, this wisp of purpose in all the surrounding, universal chaos to have value, to be worth anything at all I – we – must evade such mundane pursuits and set ourselves apart as much in the staging of that customary act as in our dress, habitation, speech or subsidiary manners.

Thus have I degraded both of us in order to set us equally as far apart from the lowly as my imagination can devise, hoping – by these indiscretions – to make us both discrete.

And you, my base precious, have never blamed me. Not for all that ravishing pain and necessary wickedness; for all that's passed your lips, not one word of abjuration has ever issued from your mouth.

Oh, you were always lost in the depths of some calm assessment, always rapt, always cloaked in the simple but engrossing business of just being yourself; I have seen the choice of morning clothes occupy you almost until lunch, been witness to the search for precisely the correct scent, watched it take an afternoon or more of delicate, dedicated anointing, slow rubbing and judicious sniffing, observed a simple sonnet absorb you for an evening of frowns and troubled sighs, found you intent and serious, the very picture of unaffected sincerity as you hang on every word of some dreadful bore for what seems half the night, and known you in your sleep, I'd swear, be roused, rutted and then resume your deeper slumbers without ever fully waking up.

Still I think you see as I do, for all our variations.

We alone are choate, we solely are ordered, while the rest – distributed, piled like grains of sand, these refugees – are but random light, a blank white hiss, an empty page, a snowed-out screen, the always renewing, ever decaying fall-out from a state of grace we may at least aspire to by our efforts.

Flapping, snapping, in the air above my musing head, I think I hear the old snow tiger's still extant exterior as, like one hand clapping, one hand waving, it salutes the night.

CHAPTER
SIX

B right morning comes; the bloody-fingered dawn with zealous light sets seas of air ablaze and bends to earth another false beginning. My eyes open like cornflowers, stick, crusted with their own stale dew, then take that light.

I stand, then haul myself up to kneel at one of the tower's narrow windows, rubbing the sleep from my eyes and gazing out to witness the dawn.

Brandished and flagrant, the sunlight strikes this dun plain and makes of it a cauldron where rising vapours multiply and summit only to, in clearness, disappear, dissolved within an oceanic waste of sky.

I take in the view while expelling my own waste, as, going

on a slow curve out, my personal contribution to the moat floats free, golden in the new-day's haze and splashing, foaming on the dark waters below, each sunstruck, brassily delineated droplet a shining stitch within a rope of gold; a glowing sine like a metaphor for light.

Lightened, I return to my makeshift bed by the side of the cold, page-clinkered grate; I intend only to rest, but fall asleep again, to be woken by the sounds of a key turning and a knock at the door.

'Sir?'

I sit up, disoriented with the hollowness arising from sleep needlessly resumed and then uncomfortably interrupted.

'Good morning, sir. I've brought some breakfast.' Old Arthur, wheezing from his journey up the narrow winding stair, squeezes through the door and deposits a tray upon a trunk. He looks apologetically at me. 'May I sit, sir?'

'Of course, Arthur.'

He collapses gratefully upon a paper-piled chair, producing a cloud of dust which circles lazily in the sunlight shafting through the broken windows of the tower. His chest heaves, his legs splay and he pulls out a handkerchief to pat and mop his brow.

'Beg your pardon, sir. Not as young as I used to be.'

There are times when there is simply nothing to be said; were someone equal to my station to pronounce such a phrase, I would select a reply with the judicious relish of a marksman in the bush who's come upon a perfect specimen of his prey, nearby and unsuspecting, and has to decide upon which gun to use. With an old and valued servant, such sport would be an impropriety, demeaning and diminishing the two of us. I have known those, mostly born to but none deserving our rank, who revel in such chances to insult those who wait and those who serve, and by all appearances derive much satisfaction from such ignoble play, but theirs is a wit born, I think, of weakness. One should only spar with those near equal to oneself, otherwise the contest tells us nothing beyond the embarrassingly obvious, and they unwittingly confirm this who in their propensity for picking on those ruled-out from replying directly expose themselves as most likely defenceless against those who could.

Besides, I know that those beneath us have their pride; they are simply ourselves in different circumstances, and those of our station allow each other self-esteem carelessly enough. We are all our own legal system, where we feel the need and see the opportunity; apprehending, judging, dispensing and, where we can, enforcing whatever by our personal philosophy we deem legitimate. The spat-out criticism of some waiter is as likely to be followed – behind the double-swing of the kitchen doors – by the favour returned, un-metaphorically, as an extra hidden sauce on the next dish, and surely many a slighted servant has nursed a grievance until able to return the contempt through well-placed gossip, or – acting on their own close-gathered intelligence of what is most precious to their tormentor – the damaging, injury, breaking or loss of that treasure. There is a nicely calculated weight of balance in such unequal relationships that is far more easy for those above to ignore than those below, but which we disregard at our peril.

Such mistake perhaps finds itself reflected and exaggerated in the distorting mirror of our present difficulties. To my present regret I never did care much for politics, even as something to despise with any knowledgeability, and so arguably speak with less authority in this than other matters, but it seems to me that the conflict now surrounding us was at least partly born in a similar lack of consideration.

There are tensions between states, peoples, races, castes and classes which any given player – individual or group – simply neglects, takes for granted or attempts to manipulate for their advantage only at the risk of their very existence and by placing in jeopardy all that they hold dear. To do so knowingly is to be foolhardy enough; to do so without such awareness is loudly to proclaim oneself an utter idiot indeed.

How many pointless tragedies, struggles-to-the-death and bloody wars have begun with the search for some small advantage, one minor piece of territory, a slight concession or minor admission, only to grow, through mutual resistance, up-welling pride and actions demanded by that self-righteous sense of justice, into an encompassing horror that altogether obliterates the very edifice the contestants sought only to amend?

Old Arthur sits, panting on the seat in the cloud of dust his sitting raised. It occurs to me that he has aged significantly in the last few months. Of course, he truly is old; by far the most venerable of our staff, and as we approach the grave I suppose the steps grow steeper. He was the only one to choose to stay with the castle rather than come with us and trust to the roads and the supposed anonymity of the fleeing displaced. We understood, and did not try too hard to persuade him otherwise; the road promised only prolonged privations, while the castle, occupied by others, offered the chance for someone of his years to take advantage of any dregs of respect the warlike young might still bestow upon the innocent old or at worst, perhaps, a quick end.

He sneezes. 'Excuse me, sir.'

'Are our guests treating you well, Arthur?'

'Me, sir?' The old fellow looks bemused.

I meant it in the plural. 'You and the other servants; are the soldiers treating you decently?'

'Ah.' He looks at his handkerchief, then blows his nose in it and folds it away. 'Yes, sir, well enough. Though they do tend to make a terrible mess.'

'I think they have lived outside, or in ruined places, for too long.'

'Sir, given it was them and their sort did the ruining in the first place,' he says, leaning closer and dropping his voice, 'perhaps that's where they belong!' He sits back, nodding but looking alarmed, as though he wishes not to take full responsibility for what his lips have just expressed.

'A good point, Arthur,' I say, amused. I swing my legs to the floor and sit up. I lift a glass of tepid milk from the tray and drink. There is toast, an egg, an apple, some preserves and a pot of coffee, which tastes tired just from the length of time it has been stored, but is still welcome.

'D'you know, sir,' Arthur says, shaking his head. 'One of them sleeps outside the lieutenant's door each night, like a dog! It's that one with the red hair; Karma I heard someone call him, or some funny name like that. I saw him last night, lying there in the doorway with just a blanket over him. Apparently he always does that wherever she is; at her feet if they're camping in the outside, sir; at her feet, just like a dog!'

'Commendable,' I say, finishing the milk. 'And they'll tell you you can't find the staff these days, eh?'

'Shall I fetch some fresh clothes, sir?' Arthur asks, smoothly resuming his professional manner. 'There are still some in the laundry.'

'I ought to wash first,' I tell him, choosing a slice of toast; the bread has been unevenly toasted, but one must become inured to such privations, I suppose. 'Is there any hot water?'

'I'll fetch some, sir. Will you be bathing in your own apartments?'

I rub my face, greasy from the day and night before. 'Am I allowed to?' I ask. 'Does our brave lieutenant consider my punishment complete?'

'I believe so, sir; she told me to take you breakfast and let you out, before she left.' His eyes widen as he takes in what I have just said. '*Punish* you, sir? *Punish* you? What right has she?' He sounds quite indignant. I have not heard his voice raised so since I was a child, and used to torment him. 'What – but – what right—? What could you do, in, in, in your home that let her—?'

'I let slip a sack of what was neither edible nor mountable,' I tell him, trying to calm him. 'But what do you mean, "left"? Where has she gone?'

Arthur sits tutting for a moment or two longer, then hauls his attention back. 'I – oh, I don't know, sir; they left – I think there's a half-dozen of them still here – the rest, the lieutenant and the rest, the ones she took, they left just after dawn. Just a handful of them still here. In search of hardware, the ones that left, that is, I think I heard one say, but that could be wrong sir; my hearing . . .' Arthur shakes his head, withered fingers trembling near one ear.

'And our good lady? Is she abroad?' I ask, smiling.

'Abroad, with them, sir,' the old servant says, expression troubled. 'The lady lieutenant . . . she took her too, as some sort of guide.'

I use the little fruit knife on the apple, silent for a while. 'Did she indeed?' I say eventually, dabbing at my lips with a napkin, clean but not, alas, pressed. 'And did they say when they expected to return?'

'I did ask, sir,' Arthur says, shaking his head. 'The lieutenant lady just said, "In good time." I'm afraid that's all I was able to get out of her.'

'Indeed,' I mutter. 'Probably no more than man can get into her.'

'I beg your pardon, sir?'

'Nothing, Arthur,' I say, letting him pour me a cup of coffee. 'Draw me a bath, will you? And if you could sort out some clothes . . .'

'Of course, sir.' He leaves me to my thoughts.

Gone, with you. A guide; some sort of guide, indeed. You, who could get lost between adjoining rooms, you to whom two hedges constitute a maze. If the lieutenant has no maps – nor any of her men a decent sense of direction – I may never see you or any of them again. The lieutenant jests, I think. You may be a mascot or a trophy to recompense her for those worthless prizes I consigned to the waters yesterday, but not, I trust, truly a guide.

But she has taken you from me. I feel a kind of jealousy, I think. How novel, considering what we've shared, one could even say disseminated. I might even think to savour this unfamiliar bouquet, at least to swill it round before I spit it out, but it has always seemed to me an ignoble emotion, a confession of moral weakness.

I feel I am reduced by her, so close to you. I fear my own seduction into a vulgar judgmentality, just the kind of facile moralism I have most despised in others.

I rise and make my way to our apartments; the pillows on your bed are piled oddly, and when I take them away, I find a pair of bullet-holes in the headboard. I replace the pillows and proceed next door to my own room. There is a smell of something burned here; perhaps old horse hair. I can find no obvious source for the odour, though when I sit on it to remove my shoes, perhaps the mattress on my bed feels different. I look up; the tassels forming the fringe of the bed's canopy appear dark and soot-stained just over where I sit. Well, there seems to be no other damage.

Arthur has the other servants bring me bowls and jugs of steaming hot water, produced by the fuel-omnivorous stove in the kitchens. The bedroom's fire is charged with logs, and lit. I bathe alone, complete my toilet and then dress before the roaring fire.

From our windows, I look out upon our other guests, those fled, shaken out from the patchwork lands about and amassed here upon our lawns with their tents and animals, their choice of campsite by itself a mute appeal for sanctuary. There was a cathedral, in a town not far away, but I understand it fell to guns some months ago. It might have been a fitter focus of attraction, but perhaps for those gathered here today the castle serves in its place; its stony existence over the years by itself somehow an augur of good fortune, a talisman guaranteeing life and charity for those nearby. I believe this is what is called a pious hope.

I conduct my own inspection of the castle. The lieutenant's men remaining are those most needing rest; the more seriously wounded, and two who may be shellshocked. I feel I ought to talk to some, and so I attempt to engage a couple of the wounded in conversation in the makeshift ward that was our ballroom.

One is a heavy-set man, prematurely grey, a jagged, ill-healed scar on his face a year or so old, who hobbles on makeshift crutches, one leg wounded by a mine which killed the man walking in front of him a week ago. The other is a shy youth, sandy haired and of a pale and flawless complexion. He has a bullet in one shoulder, all strapped and bandaged; his chest is smooth and hairless. He seems sweet, seductive even, made more so by his air of injured vulnerability. I think, in another time, we might both have taken to this one.

I do my best, but in both cases each of us is awkward; the older man is by turns taciturn and garrulous – angry, I suspect, at whatever he considers I represent – while the boy is merely wincingly demure and diffident, his long-lashed eyes averted. I am more at ease with the servants, sharing their mixture of quiet horror and unfeigned amusement at the uncouthness of the soldiers. They seem happy just to be busy again, returned to their purpose and taking solace in the familiarity of duty and service. I make a remark about keeping occupied that meets with politeness rather than genuine appreciation.

I take a stroll through the grounds. The people in the camp seem almost as tongue-tied as the soldiers. Many of them are sick; I am told a child died yesterday. I meet the wife of the village Factor tending a fire by one of the tents; we saw her husband yesterday on the road when the lieutenant intercepted us. She and he live here, for now. He has gone with the other fit men of the camp in search of more food, hoping to plunder farms already ransacked many times.

I feel I should be doing something assertive, dynamic; I ought to make my own escape, try to bribe the soldiers still in the castle, attempt to form the servants into a resistance or rouse the people of the camp . . . but I think I do not have the character required for such heroics. My talents lie in other directions. Were some barbed comment all that was required to wrest and maintain control in this, I might leap to action and emerge victorious. As it is, I see too many options and possibilities, arguments and counter-arguments, objections and alternatives. Lost within a mirror-maze of tactical potential, I see everything and nothing, and lose my way in images. Men of iron find their soul contaminated, their purpose corroded in the presence of a surfeit of irony.

I retire to the castle, climb to the battlements and by the tower – the same one in which I was imprisoned last night – inspect the trio the lieutenant had suspended here. They sway in a damp breeze, uniforms flapping. The dark hoods over their heads, I see now, are pillow slips of black silk, where often our heads have lain. The moist fabric clings to their features, turning their faces into sculptures of jet. Two of them, arms dangling tied behind, have their chins on their chests as though gazing morosely down at the moat. The head of the third man is thrown back, his hands clutching the rope at his neck, his fingers pressed between the rope and black-bruised skin, one leg drawn up behind his rear, his back still arched and his whole body frozen in that last desperate posture of agony. Behind the black silk, his eyes look open, staring up at the sky, accusatory.

It seems unfair; all they did was try to unearth some booty in a building abandoned by its owners, not expecting to incur the lieutenant's vengeful wrath. She says it was to make a point, to provide an example, by initial ruthlessness to make a more lenient regime the easier to maintain.

Above them, on the flagpole, the old snow-tiger skin ruffles heavy in the gentle wind. The two rear leg-pieces have been crudely tied to the lanyard, the skin itself looks worn and thinned in places, it is matted with the rain that's visited us over the last few days and still troubles the distances of plain, and in all is just too weighty for the use the lieutenant's men have tried to press it to. A stiff breeze will hardly lift it, a strong wind will make it snap and sail all right, but much more – a decent gust – and I suspect it will snap the flagpole too.

It seems an ignominious end for this aged heirloom, but how else would the old thing have ended its days? Thrown out upon a midden, burned in some bonfire? Perhaps this is a more fitting end.

It stirs itself in the curling breeze, and looses a few anointing drops of soaked-up rain upon the bodies hanging under it.

The cold weather means the lieutenant's trophies have not yet started to smell. I leave them and the furry flag to their fixed contemplation of all things pendulous and pending and walk along the serried summit of the castle.

From these brave battlements with a chosen bird of prey I used to fly my spirit free. From this quarried perch, I as much as the quarry they seized was gripped by them, and through those sleek carnivores, swift death's craftsmen, I felt that I partook of their airborne, slicing skill, and saw, in that stooping instant of mortality, a kind of ephemeral persistence. Here were the old rules, written across the sky in dark, gliding purpose, in curved lines of flight, in the panicking dips and flips and desperate lunges, dives and sprints of the target, all answered by instant flicks and turns executed by the following, closing hawk. Here was the sudden buffeting connection – sometimes, close enough, you heard the thud of talons hitting flesh – the small puff of feathers that hung upon the air, then the long, corkscrewing fall, the raptor's wings scrabbling for purchase in the air, its prey limp or struggling weakly, also flapping, and the whole, this binary avian creation – one dead or dying, the other more alive than ever before, as though transfused – that death-melded twin secured by claw and tendon, rotating about their shared axis as they dropped locked together, drizzling feathers, distributing the game's last plaintive cries and then falling finally to field, lawn or wood.

The dogs were trained to frighten off the hawks, then with their warm cargo come running back to the castle, across the stone moat bridge, through the courtyard, up the winding stair

85

and out on to the battlements, a trail of feathers and blood behind them on the spiralled steps.

With those surrogate hunters I sought to be part of that ruthlessly elegant struggle of life and death, evolution and selection, predator and prey. I believed I might, through them, withstand the air's stern siege and the slow weathering of time and the onward tramp of age, by meeting it with no cloud's means – giving way and giving in – but a carving use instead; a fixity of vision and of grasp that would let me – so delegated, unreduced – stand, connected and defined.

The dogs died last year; some illness when there was no vet to be found. Generations of devotion and meticulous breeding went with them.

I let the damn birds go when first we left the castle, fleeing from a fate that instead found us, and where they sail now, what they see and take, I cannot know.

The wind wraps me, the wind comes to me and leaves across the beaten plains. Slim slivers of sunlight prise underneath the clouds and, reflecting, appear to take instead of give, dazzling like camouflage, by their jarring contrast, bright on dark, breaking up the few remaining shapes and signs of civilisation still evident, in better light (like that the memory provides), within the steady chaos of the landscape's reach.

Within the fields, the outcrop hills and the stands of trees, the stagnant oxbows gleam with a soiled yellow grace, alive to the eye from this angle only. The trees, lately coloured within the season's slow turn chill, now are bared black shapes, branches bared for the weight of snow and the force of winter storm. Higher, the forests glisten with the clouds that slew above them and about, and snag their slow grace down.

I listen for the sound of artillery, but the freshened wind has quartered, and holds the gunfire back. That distant, artificial thunder has become an almost comforting companion over these last weeks. It is as though we have relapsed into a more primitive system of belief, as though by the fractious meddling with our collective, lived-through histories we have woken one of the old gods; a storm god, one to stride, hammer-footed, anvil-headed over the land, amorphous, angry and omnipresent, while thunder like the sound of cracking skulls splits over all our darkened lands and the air conducts the lightning's breath to earth.

That woken deity marches on us now, towards the castle's doors. The noise is like the earth's gut rumbling, like an old fist slamming empty boards in an abandoned heaven overhead, and for all that the freshened wind has formed its own front against the blast, and moving air displaced all that noise, we know it is still there; what wind conceals, the mind insists upon revealing, providing the memory of that sound.

Air and rock, even the seas, forget quicker than we do.

A shout in the mountains fades over seconds, the earth itself rings like a bell when its sliding and colliding continents spasm, but that signal too fades over days, and for all that great storm-waves and long tsunami can circle round the globe for weeks and months, our modest lump of stem-flowered brain quite outdoes such crudely mechanical recollection, and what echoes in the human skull may resonate for a long lifetime of joy, fear or regret, only over decades slowly decaying.

Squinting against the barrage of light, in the distance I believe I can make out a few moving forms, frames made skinny, elongated against the ricocheting brightness of the reflecting water. I have no binoculars or spotting scopes left – they have been requisitioned – but either would be worse than useless, staring into this already painful light. Are those refugees I see, implicit in the shimmer of shadows against light? They could be soldiers, I suppose; they might even be you, my dear, leading our lieutenant and her men on an unintentional wild-goose-chase, but I think not. It might have been a herd of cattle, up to a few months ago, but most beasts hereabouts have been killed and eaten since, and the few that remain are closely watched and not allowed to wander.

Refugees, then; a pre-echo of the coming front, the very image of the deep, soughing trough before the great wave falls, an in-drawn breath before the scream; a rush of dead cells in these arterial ways, a scramble of dry leaves before the coming storm. Bared and broken trees line their way, the splintered stumps, the pale heart-wood naked to the air; hacked, torn down for camp fires as though by massed gunfire. They stand, grown but broken, in imitation of their fretful mutilators.

The light changes, dimming the brash coruscations of the view. The river, tributaries, drainage ditches, oxbows, pools and flooded fields dim as the clouds shut off their direct source of sun. Now I can see some thin parings of smoke rising from the plain, marking where villages, farms and houses were, the dwellings built from, growing on and taking in the land and all its separated product now combining with the barren air.

I look for you, my dear, our lieutenant and her men, but all is lost within the fractured surface of the view, all is foundered in its prostrate complexity, and the sintered land has you absorbed.

And so I stamp these stones, I walk this elevated way, I rub my hands and watch my breath like a warning go out before me, and can only wait.

I am cold; I gather phlegm in my throat and send it too towards the moat, then smile at that encircling water. There, like leaves scattered by the autumn wind, like those wasting cells again, and like the dispossessed who clogged up all our roads, I see the downward filtered, the long way travelled, the by-that-stream transported finches; the birds we shot and I lost, all dead and wet, bedraggled, cold and slowly turning in our sustaining ring of water. Our dead chicks, come home to roost at last.

CHAPTER
SEVEN

The night comes to the castle, and I return to sleep. My dreams, my dearest, take the same direction as my last conscious thoughts, turning to you, still unreturned. Such reveries tease from my mind the old, lascivious memories – summoned up, swelling from the depths, by the mounting pleasures they recall.

I search for you in my dreams, stumbling through a landscape of desire where clouds and snowdrifts become pillows, a stroked cheek, pale heavy breasts. Submerging in hidden, fern-fringed clefts, surrendering to the clinging pool and its sweetly bitter perfume, I see trees that rear, tumescent, from curved collected veins of roots; smooth fissured rocks in plunging gorges; rearing stems pulsing with sap and life; downy fruits, fallen and creviced; rifts cracked in the earth itself surrounded by stony crests and crowns, and become aware that every feature hides something craved. Worshipping before and lusting after, I find myself half-lost, as though by your nature already partially infected.

I would possess this land; I want to take it, make it mine, but I cannot. The water remains water, nothing else, the towering trees stay just trees; fruits rot, and the stones, smooth and curved, seem to promise something if only they could be lifted, prized away . . . but they will not be moved.

All that's to be done is toss and turn in this too-big bed; before now, in similar circumstances, I would have ascended to a higher level and gone in search of a compliant maid or other servant with whom to while away the night, but we have only men left in our employ these days; nothing to excite in those hired hands.

Adrift on this raft of bed, I roll abandoned in my dreams like a ship without way, pitched and driven by swell and gust, your body a distant memory, like a misty glimpse of land.

Then, by a strange reversal, the image the reality creates. Our brave lieutenant has returned, and sent you to me, to creep quietly into my bed and slip between these sheets. I turn in my sleep and it turns into wakefulness; you kneel, then lie, still silent. I hold you close, my open one. You stare, half clothed, at the bed's dark canopy overhead. Light – bipartisan, cast by the fire dying in the grate and a steady wash of moonlight pouring through one window – exposes a flush upon your cheek. Your skin and hair are heady with the scent of open air, and your long black, let-down hair hangs heavy and bejewelled with bits of twigs and torn scraps of leaves.

Your eyes have that broken, careless look I remember from

when first we met. Watching them from one side, I feel that now I see more in them than I have at any time since. Sometimes only the sideways view tells true; the selves, the faces we manufacture for the world to ease our passage through it are too used to frontal assault, and I think that I see more truth in you just now than ever I did enquiring straight. I suppose I should have known; what has our shared taste taught us if not that the interest's more, when taken oblique?

'Are you all right?' I ask.

You wait, then nod.

The lieutenant's men sound noisy in the yard; engines rattle down to silence, rifles fall, lights shiver beyond the drawn curtains, shouts echo round the castle's walls like voices from the stones, and the castle, more than we, seems to breathe around us.

I persist. 'How did the day go?'

Another hesitation. 'Well enough.'

'Is there anything you want to tell me?'

You shift your head minimally and look at me. 'What would you like to know?'

'Where you've been. What happened.'

'I have been with Loot,' you tell me, looking away. I try to raise my hand to you, but it is caught beneath the tangled bedclothes. I have to shift across the bed, grunting, to free it from the knot of clothes. 'We drove across to the hills on the far side,' you continue. I have my hand free now, but cannot raise the wrath to strike you. I may have ascribed you too much wit anyway. '. . . been with Loot.' It could have meant no more than the most innocent interpretation. And besides, I now recall, I have resolved not to be jealous. I smooth the now freed hand through my hair, then yours, loosing fragments of twigs to fall upon the pillow.

'Did anything happen?' I ask.

'They found a goat, tied to a stake in one farm. In another there was a tank of diesel which they tried to drain but could not. They shot the tank to fill some containers from the hole but discovered it held only water. There was a place they think was an orphanage, to the west. I had not heard of it. The children had all been crucified.'

'Crucified?' I ask, frowning.

'On telegraph poles. On the road outside. Twenty or more, all down the road. I lost count. I was crying.'

'Who could have done that?'

'They did not know.' You turn to me. 'The next man they met on that road, they shot. All of them; all at once. He was walking away and had some cans of food they thought he must have taken from the orphanage. He said he had not noticed the children but they could see he was lying.'

'And after that?'

'They found a quarry in the hills, a dynamite store, but it was empty.'

'Then what?'

'They talked to people on the road; refugees. They threatened them but did not harm them, were told something they wanted to know. We went up into the hills, on a track. I think we passed the Anders' house. Some of them went ahead, taking horses from a farm there, and the rest went on foot. I was left with two of them at the jeeps. They all came back later without having found anything. It had been night for some time by then. Too dark.'

'And after that?'

'We made our way back. Oh, we crossed a bridge over the river, and there were boats with dead people in them; one of their scouts had seen them yesterday. They dragged the boats ashore and hid them, in case they ever had to use them later. The dead people they let float down the river. That was on the way back here.'

'An eventful day.'

You nod. The fire throws wavering shadows across the ornately corniced ceiling and the dark, wood-panelled walls.

'An eventful day,' you whisper, agreeing.

I say nothing for a while. 'Were you all right?' I ask eventually. 'Did the lieutenant treat you properly?'

You are silent for a long time. The fire shadows dance. Eventually, you say: 'With all the deference and esteem that I have come to expect.'

I am not sure what to say. So I say nothing. I attend, instead, to our situation. Still you lie and I look, and – watching, lying – steady we remain, as though in that moment timeless.

But we are never so; my thoughts contradict their own genesis. Time itself is not timeless, much less us. We are willing victims of our own quickness, and, while the more elegant action might have been to turn my back, ignoring you, I did not. Instead I reached out, I made an effort, and for a chosen moment decided to decide no more, and, guided by a coarser, simpler layer of mind to act as well, reached over, gripped the bedclothes' edge, and covered you.

I dreamt of summer in my reinstated sleep, of a time, many years ago, when our liaison was new and fresh and still a secret, or so we thought, and you and I went on a picnic, riding horses to a distant meadow in the wooded hills.

Such energetic canterings always excited you, and we rode again, you facing me, straddling and impaled, your skirts covering our union, while that brave horse, uncomplaining, rode round and round within the hidden, sunlit arena of that flower-carpeted, insect-loud clearing, the animal's springing, muscled vigour bringing us, finally, eventually, by our relative stillness (hypnotised, oblivious, lost within that lengthened moment of dappling light and buzzing air) surrendering all control to its long pulsing motions, to a sweet mutuality of bliss.

While always preferring poetic injustice to prosaic probity, it would, I think, have been a shame if that which wakened us in the morning had put us instantly back to sleep again, so that, in some state, we lay in.

You were always the darker sleeper; I have seen your slow unslumbering take more than one cock's crow to achieve. Our reveille is accomplished, however, by something capable of flight which happily does not find its voice.

Sudden and intrusive chaos takes the castle's roof, its floors, walls and our room and shakes it all; flaps the castle's stones like a scaly flag and sets free the dust and us, tumultuous and milling and emplaced within its cloud, losing us within that swirling, particulate confusion.

A shell; a first too-lucky round that found the castle out and hit it square, running it through, producing a violent trail of stone dust, splintered wood and panic in its wake. But to no climax; it stops between the ground and lower floors, unexploded.

I reassure you as you sob, reduced to patting and uttering trite inanities by this unexpected intrusion. I look around at the dry mist of choking dust the shell's passage has bestowed upon us, while an arid shower of debris patters from the hole in the ceiling on to the floor, then I go calm and smiling from you, a kerchief held over my nose, waving white clouds aside, to inspect the demolished corner of my room. There is a hole above, and daylight visible through curling dust. The upper part of the wall has been removed in a great semicircle, as though bitten by a giant, affording a view into a dark space next door. It should be an old storeroom, piled high with furniture, if I recall correctly. Beyond would be the principal guests' suite, which the lieutenant has commandeered for her own use.

I climb upon the side of an elegant armoire – it escaped injury by a hand's breadth as the shell passed it by – and lean into the shadows on the far side of the stone and rubble wall. Stretching forward and reaching through, past age-dark, torn wood, I detect an odd chemical smell; an odour from my childhood which I associate with clothes, parties and with hiding. I see something metallic glint and reach for it. Mothballs; the scent is of mothballs, I think suddenly.

My hand closes round a coat-hanger. I pull it from its rail, in the punctured wardrobe standing in the dim room beyond, then throw it back and climb back down. Below my feet, another hole leads through the mosaic of wooden flooring, boards, lathe and plaster into the dusty dining-room. Shouts issue from the gap, and the sound of running feet.

I go to the windows and open them to the day, leaving the curtains drawn behind me. A curious peace reigns beyond; another ordinary day, with mist and a low, watery sun. Birds sing in the woods. 'What are you doing?' you wail from the bed. 'I'm cold!'

I lean out, looking up to the skies – at this point still thinking that we might have been bombed rather than shelled – then out towards the hills and the plain. 'I think the windows are safer open, if we are to be bombarded,' I tell you. 'If you like, being underneath the bed might be advisable.' I look for my clothes, but they were left on a seat that stood where our little visitor has passed; on the floor by the hole I find a few kindling-sized bits of the seat itself and a couple of buttons from my jacket. I wind myself in a white sheet, pour dust out of my shoes and slip them on, then catch sight of myself in a mirror and kick the shoes off again. I descend to meet the others, thinking to follow the artillery round's route down through the castle.

In the Long Room on the floor below the lieutenant's men run shouting, clutching weapons or their pants. A dulling whoop from outside the walls makes us all duck or dive. There follows an equivocal sort of thud, something that neither ears nor feet want to take full responsibility for sensing, a conclusion that the brain may have provided by itself. We rise, and I walk on.

In the dining-room, its generous depths extended by the dust which fills it, two soldiers wave their arms over a hole in the floor which must lead down to the kitchens or cellars. Above, the punctured roof rains powdery motes. From a tear in the ceiling close by, a thin pipe hangs free, wagging; steaming water geysers from it, splashing down upon the table and the central rug, steam contending with the corkscrewing weight of dust. Curtains, caught by a piece of fallen frieze work, lie sprawled on the floor, admitting light which catches the dust and steam. I stop for a moment, forced to admire this fabulous disarray.

As I approach the hole and the two soldiers, a huge tearing noise, braided with a dying, inhuman scream, rips across the sky outside; the two irregulars throw themselves to the floor, thudding to raise more dust. I stand, looking at them. This time there is an explosion; sound bursts in the distance, quaking the boards beneath my feet and rattling the windows like a storm's gust. I run to the windows as the lieutenant's men scramble to their feet. Peering out, I can see nothing, just the same calm skies.

I take a look down the hole the soldiers are now kneeling by, then head for the corridor outside, tiptoeing across a shallow pool of warm water.

'A ghost already?' says the lieutenant's voice. I turn and she is there, long boots thudding down the stairs two at a time, pulling on a jacket, tousle-headed, stuffing a thick green shirt into her fatigues, a holstered pistol at her hip. She looks tired, as though just woken from the very depths of sleep, and yet more consummate too, as if all chaos merely served to boil excess water from her spirit and leave a stronger concentration behind.

'Mr Cuts!' she yells, over me, to her deputy just appeared at the far end of the Long Room. 'Onetrack on guard? Send Deathwish and Poppy up there too; see if they can spot where this stuff's coming from. Tell them to keep their heads down and watch the grounds too in case it's cover. And get Ghost on the radio; find out if he can see anything from the gatehouse.' She sticks her head round the door to the dining-room. 'Dopple!' she calls out. 'Fix that leak; get one of the servants to show you where the stopcocks are.' She waves dust from in front of her face, then sneezes, and for the smallest moment is girlish, a soft but hard figure in this haphazard mist shaken from the castle's strength.

'Oh, sir!' Rolans, one of our younger staff, a pasty-faced young man of an awkward, chubby build, comes running up to me, struggling into a jacket. 'Sir, what—?'

'You'll do,' the lieutenant says, grabbing the fellow by his wrist. She urges him towards the soldier emerging from the dining-room. 'Here you are, Dopple; go and do some plumbing.'

The one she called Dopple grunts. Rolans looks at me; I nod. The two set off along the corridor, whitened faces like badges

in the morning gloom. The desiccated smoke that is the stone
and plaster dust rolls about them, contaminating all of us – as
we move and breathe within that everywhere surface – with
an infection of the castle's assaulted shock, leaving us all half
ghosts and I, in my blank uniform, archly archetypal.

The lieutenant turns to a man limping past wearing a steel
helmet and carrying a rifle, puts out one arm across his chest
and brings him smoothly to a stop. He looks frightened; sweat
coats his face save where a long jagged scar runs. It is the elder
of the two men I spoke to yesterday. 'Victim,' she says, gently
(and I have to think, well, he was at least well named). 'Easy,
now. Get the wounded down to the cellars on the east side of
the castle, would you?'

He swallows, nods, and limps quickly off.

I look after him. 'I'm not sure that's the safest place,' I tell
her. 'I think that first shell ended up in one of the cellars.'

'Let's take a look, shall we?'

'Is that safe?' I ask as the lieutenant ignites her lighter in the
darkness.

She looks at me in its flickering yellow flame. Her mouth
takes on a small twist. 'Yes,' she says shortly. We are in the
cellars squatting on top of an empty concrete coal bunker,
gazing at a pile of rubble fallen from the ceiling and landed on
top of a log-pile; my toga-garb makes the position awkward
and my feet must be filthy.

The lieutenant takes her silver cigarette case from her jacket,
selects and lights a cigarette. I feel I am being treated to a show
of courage. She draws upon it languidly, breathes out.

'I meant,' I find myself saying, 'that we are in a fuel store.'
It sounds lame. I hope the lighter flame is too weak to show
my blush.

The lieutenant looks sceptical, glancing about the dark cellar. 'Anything explosive in here?'

'Only that, I suppose.' I indicate the pile of rubble where we are assuming the shell has come to rest.

'Unlikely,' she says, drawing upon the cigarette. 'Here; hold this,' I am told. I am given the lighter. The light is poor. How odd the things one misses. I am trying to remember the last time I saw a torch battery. The lieutenant leans forward, cigarette jammed in the corner of her mouth, and scrapes some of the debris carefully away, sending small soft falls of pale dust spilling softly to the floor of the coal-black room. Some shards of rock follow, then she tugs and hauls, grunting, at a more reluctant piece. There is an alarming crunch and a small raft of dusty stone and broken wood collapses off the wineracks, taking some logs with it.

'Hold the light closer,' she tells me. I do so. 'Ha,' she says, supporting herself on the underside of the ceiling as she leans forward to jostle something out of the way above. 'There it is.' I look, and see the swollen side of a gleaming metal casing. She smooths dust from its flank, hand gentle as any mother's on her child's head. 'Two-ten,' she breathes. A tremor shakes the cellar around us, and the sound of a distant explosion comes through the hole to the dining-room above. The lieutenant sits back, slapping her hands, seemingly unheeding. 'Better get at it from above.'

The lieutenant watches as two men pick at the shell's brief tomb, kneeling on the dining-room's splintered floor and reaching down to scoop out lumps of stone and wood. The flow from the water pipe hanging over the dining table has been reduced to a drip; water has pooled towards the room's outer wall, forming a long, gently steaming pool. Above, one of the servants is attempting to repair the void in my bedroom floor, gagging its throat with wood and an old mattress; his efforts dislodge more clouds of falling, rolling dust. Every now and again pieces of plaster fall from the hole, hitting the floor near us like small powdery bombs.

A noise behind us is the red-haired soldier, treading with a comic wariness over the film of dust on the floor and holding something long and black. He approaches the lieutenant, makes a sort of half bow to her and mutters something, handing her the garment. It is a long black opera cloak, red to the inside. I think it was Father's. She smiles as the soldier backs off, and thanks him. She glances at me with a look of amused tolerance, then puts it on, opening it and swinging it out so that it settles over her shoulders like a shadow.

Another plaster-bomb plummets from the ceiling, crashing on to the floor beside the two men clearing the rubble away from the shell and making them jump. They glance round, then continue. The lieutenant glares up, hand waving in front of her face.

'So much dust,' she says.

I gaze upwards too. 'Indeed. But then the place has had four centuries to dry out.'

She merely grunts, then claps her hands, releasing dust, and in a small storm of it swirls out in her dramatic cloak, her footprints upon our punctured, coated floor like an animal's in snow.

Still clad in my sheet, I stand, trying not to shiver, on the battlements with the lieutenant and a group of her men. She puts down the field-glasses. 'No sign,' she says. Her stubby fingers tap on the stonework, her eyes narrow as she takes in the distant scene.

The artillery fire has stopped and left the morning hung out as though to dry, its dew hanging from the smooth ridges and the needled trees like a coy veil the land's assumed following the distant gun's intolerant assault. There have been no more shells for ten minutes or so. The last was the closest – excluding that first which pierced the castle – landing in the woods up-hill one hundred metres off. A faint wisp of smoke rises from where it hit, though there is no other obvious damage to the forest. The men the lieutenant sent to the roof were not able to observe where the shells were coming from. They confer, trying to agree how many rounds were fired. They settle on six, with at least two of them duds. There is some talk concerning who fired upon us and from where. The lieutenant sends two of the men below and stands leaning on the parapet, gazing towards the hills.

'You know who might be firing at us?' I ask. My feet are numb but I want to find out what I can.

She nods, not looking at me. 'Yes. Old friends of ours.' She takes another cigarette from her case, lights it. 'We tried to take the gun that fired it a week or two ago, but they have it in the hills now.' She pulls on the cigarette.

'And in that range, appear to have ours,' I offer with a smile.

She looks at me, unimpressed. 'I think we almost found them again yesterday,' she says, and shrugs. 'Thought they'd headed off. Looks like they didn't. Must know where we are. Trying to get us to quit this place.'

I let the silence run on for another two lungfuls of smoke, then ask her, 'What will you do?'

Another draw on the cigarette. She taps some ash down towards the moat and inspects the cigarette's burning end carefully. Something about the way she does this chills me, as though our lieutenant is used to checking that such a glowing tip is just right for applying to an interrogatee's flesh. 'I think', she says contemplatively, 'we might have to take it from them.'

'Ah. I see.'

'We need that gun; destroyed, or for our own use. We have to take the thing, or leave here.' She turns to me with that thin smile. 'And I don't want to leave.' She looks away again. 'We have a rough idea where they might be; I'm sending some of the guys out to recce.' She leans on her elbows, arms straight out on front of her, hands together. She inspects the gold and ruby ring on her smallest finger, then fixes her gaze on me again. 'I might want you to look at some maps with me later on,' she says, eyes narrowing. I make no reaction. 'Found a few in the library,' she continues, 'but some of the tracks didn't seem to match up when we went looking out to the west, yesterday.'

'They're rather old maps,' I concede. 'If it's the Anders' estate, they changed quite a lot of the routes through the forest over the years. They put in new bridges, dammed one of the rivers; various things.'

'Would you know much about all that, Abel?' she asks, trying to sound casual but scratching her head.

'Sufficient to be your guide, you mean?'

'Mm-hmm.' She pulls on the cigarette again, then flicks it towards the moat. There are still some finches floating there against the banks. I'm not sure whether she's noticed or not.

'I imagine so,' I say.

'You'll do it? Be our guide?'

'Why not?' I say, shrugging.

'It'll be dangerous.'

'As might staying here be.'

'Yes; good point.' She looks me up and down. 'I'll let

you get dressed now. Meet me in the library in ten minutes.'

Ten minutes, to attend to one's toilet and dress? My face, I
think, must betray me.

'Okay,' she says, sighing. 'Twenty minutes.'

It takes a little longer than that, though I think I dress more
quickly than I ever have, save when there's been some pressing
incentive, such as the sounds indicating the unexpected return
of a notoriously jealous husband.

It is your fault, initially, my dear. When I return to our apartments you are in your own room, gasping for breath, hunting through drawers for an inhaler. You cough and wheeze,
struggling with each intake of air. An old condition; asthma
troubled you from childhood. Dust or shock might each have
brought it on again. I do my best to comfort you, but then
there is further commotion, and a frenzied hammering at
the door.

'Sir, oh sir!' Lucius, another servant, stumbles in when I give
him permission. 'Sir, sir; Arthur!'

I follow Lucius' heels up the spiral steps to the attic floor.
I suppose I should have thought; old Arthur's room is somewhere above ours, directly in line with the course the shell
took. I have a few moments to imagine what we might find.

A small room, eaved; bright wallpaper, half hidden by
settling dust. Some cheap-looking furniture. I don't think I
have been in this room ever before; it has always been the
old servant's. It must have been quite dull. There is a skylight,
but most of the illumination comes from the ragged hole in
the sloped ceiling, not far from the door, where the artillery
round passed; the hole leading to my chamber is almost at
my feet.

Arthur lies on his side in his narrow bed at the far end of the room, seemingly uninjured. He is turned towards us, propped up a little by one arm and the pillows behind him, and yet at the same time slumped. He is wearing pyjamas. A jar containing his false teeth sits on a small bedside table, beside a book on which rest his glasses. His face looks grey, and wears an expression of annoyed concentration, as though he is looking down at the floor by the bed trying to remember where he put a book, or what he's done with his glasses. Lucius and I stand in the doorway. In the end it is I who go forward, stepping over the hole in the carpeted floor.

Old Arthur's wrist is cold and without a pulse. There is a layer of what feels like talcum powder on his skin. I blow on his face, removing a patina of white dust. The skin beneath is still grey. I look apologetically at Lucius and slide my hand in under the covers towards the old fellow's belly, grimacing. It is cool under here, too.

Around his neck is a thin gold chain. Rather than a religious emblem or other lucky charm, it supports only a small, ordinary key. I slip the chain over his head and let its cool weight pool in my palm. I put it in my jacket pocket.

Arthur's eyes are still partially open; I place my fingers on the lids and close them, then press his body by one shoulder so that he flops slowly on to his back in an attitude generally regarded as more befitting the recently deceased.

I rise, shaking my head. 'A heart attack, I imagine,' I tell Lucius, looking at the hole in the roof. 'I dare say it must have been a rude awakening.' Feeling the gesture is required somehow, I pull the bed's top sheet over Arthur's grey, still face. 'Sleep on,' I find myself murmuring.

Lucius makes an odd noise, and when I look at him he is sobbing.

*   *   *

108

I return to you, my dear, en route to my rendezvous with the lieutenant, half expecting to find you wheezing blue-faced on the floor and clutching at your throat, but – like and unlike our quick visitor, and our old servant – you too now sleep.

CHAPTER
EIGHT

When I go down to meet our lieutenant, the soldiers are in the hall, watching the shell, now disinterred, going out, carried on a stretcher. Its pallid bearers handle the solid deadness of it with a facsimile of respect even more faithful than that they reserve for their leader. Baby-small and tenderly, precisely as though those who bear it are transporting someone they do not wish to wake, the shell leaves slowly, to be dumped somewhere in the woods. I make a mental note to inquire precisely where, on the off-chance we might survive to see peace again, then go on my way, to the library and the lieutenant.

I enter the library's wall-thick dimness by its already open

door and step into the silence with due deference. The lieutenant sits in an ancient chair, her head lying on her green-shirted
arms, folded on the table in front of her. The opera cloak has
been discarded, draped like a fold of night across the back of
the seat behind her. A map of our lands lies crumpled beneath
her head, her curled, bedraggled hair hovering like a dark cloud
above us all. Her eyes are closed, her mouth open slightly; she
looks like any woman sleeping, and less remarkable than most.
The ring on her small finger glints faintly.

How many devotees of Morpheus we have this morning. I
feel a small moment of power over the sleeping lieutenant,
thinking that I could reach between that old opera cloak
and her shirt and slip her automatic pistol from its holster,
threaten her, kill her, take her hostage so that her men are
forced to leave the castle, or perhaps by the boldness of my
action compel them to recognise me as the stronger leader and
agree to follow me.

But I think not. We each have our position, our place, as
much in these martial matters as in anything else and perhaps
more so.

It would, anyway, be underhand, even ungallant.

And besides, I might make a mess of it.

An atlas, old and heavy, lies by the lieutenant's head, opened
at this place. I lift one dusty side and let it fall. The thud, flat and
resonant, awakens her. She rubs her eyes and stretches, sitting
back in the creaking chair and casually, unthinkingly, placing
her boots on the table by the map. These are not army boots,
nor are they the ones she wore when we first met her; they are
long riding boots, of soft brown shining leather, a little worn
but still good. They look like an old pair of mine, the last ones I
ever outgrew; another pair of refugees abducted from our past,
no doubt exhumed from some cupboard, store or long-sealed

114

room. I watch small flakes of mud fall from their soles to caress the map. 'Ah, Abel,' the lieutenant says as I find another chair and sit across from her. Inelegant in waking as in sleep, she grinds a finger in one ear, inspects the waxened end, then her watch, and frowns. 'Better late than never.'

'The lateness is not all mine; our eldest servant has just died.'

She looks concerned. 'What, old Arthur? How?'

'The shell passed through his room. He was uninjured but I believe his heart gave out.'

'I'm sorry,' she says, taking her boots off the table, her frown still there but troubled, even sympathetic. 'I take it he'd been here a long time.'

'All of my life,' I tell her.

She makes a strange little noise with her mouth. 'I thought we'd got away unscathed, there. Damn.' She shakes her head.

I begin to feel a fractious annoyance at her sympathy and seeming sorrow. If anyone ought to feel aggrieved it is I; he was my servant and she has no right to assume my role in this, even if I have chosen not to play it to its limits; it is my right to underplay it, but not hers to understudy me.

'Well, no; we were scathed,' I say curtly. 'I'm sure he'll be much missed,' I add. (Who will bring me my breakfasts in future?)

She nods thoughtfully. 'Is there anyone we should try to inform?'

I had not even thought. I wave one hand quickly. 'I think he had some relations, but they lived at the other end of the country.' The lieutenant nods, understanding. The other end of the country; in the present circumstances one might as well say on the moon. 'Certainly there was nobody nearby,' I tell her.

'I'll see he's buried, if you like,' she offers.

I can think of a host of replies to this, but restrict myself to a nod and, 'Thank you.'

'Now.' She breathes deeply, stands, strides to the windows and pulls the curtains open to the sky. 'These maps,' she says, settling into the chair again.

We discuss her miniature campaign; she wishes to strike this afternoon, before we lose the light. The day seems fair, and without such luxuries as weather forecasts, soldiers as much as anybody else are reduced to the sort of weather lore that has apocryphally guided shepherds through the ages; best to attack when one can, lest rains set in and make the whole proceeding sodden as well as lethal.

I am what help I can be. I pencil in amendments to the charts, ploughing a new track here, erecting a bridge with a couple of pencil strokes and by a single solid line and a few wags of the wrist constructing a dam and filling in the waters behind. The lieutenant is appreciative, hmm-ing and nodding and biting on one fingernail as we talk the matter through. A curious and novel feeling of what I believe must be usefulness creeps over me, along with the surprisingly agreeable appreciation of what it is to be in a team such as that the lieutenant has around her to command, each man depending on this sort of planning, each life hanging on how well or ill she thinks through what she might ask them together to accomplish. How collective, how even convivial, if also potentially humbling as well as deadly; such exemplary *esprit de corps* makes the contrived camaraderie of the hunt look a pale and paltry thing indeed.

Later her deputy, Mr Cuts, joins us, and he too sits and studies the maps, listening to what she proposes. Mr Cuts looks to be of late middle-age; not quite old enough to be the lieutenant's father. He is tall and spindly with silvery-dark hair and wears small thin-rimmed glasses sitting high on a great narrow hook of nose.

He is, now I think of it, the only one of the lieutenant's men who is free of facial hair (even if, in the case of some of them, such hair is scarcely more than downy, youthful tufts). I was myself briefly bearded when we lost mains power a year or more ago. For this last year I've used an antique cut-throat razor old Arthur discovered for me – complete with brush, mug, mirror, whetstone and leather strop – in a storeroom. I find myself wondering if Mr Cuts has a supply of razor-blades, and whether his nickname is linked somehow to his clean-shaven nature.

The fellow sits hunched, concentrating on the maps. He contributes his own grunts and a few suggestions, mostly regarding his pessimistic projections of the distances their vehicles can cover without running out of fuel.

In time I am dismissed, albeit with the lieutenant's apparently sincere thanks. I feel excluded, perhaps denied the witnessing of their more detailed plans by an instinctive or suspicious urge in them to keep their preparations secret, perhaps by the lieutenant mistakenly thinking I might be bored by such martial business. I stop at the library door, decided.

'You're short of fuel?' I ask.

The lieutenant looks up, glancing at Mr Cuts. 'Well, yes,' she says, as though amused. 'Sort of the way everybody is, these days.'

'I know where there is some,' I tell her.

'Where?'

'Beneath our carriage, in the stables. There are a few drums of petrol and diesel and one of oil, strapped underneath.'

She looks at me, one eyebrow hoisted.

'I thought to use it as currency,' I explain, refusing to be bashful. 'Something to bargain with, while on the road.' I give a small frown and gesture with one hand. 'But please; feel free.' I smile as graciously as I can.

The lieutenant breathes slowly in and out. 'Well, that's very generous of you, Abel,' she says. Her eyes narrow above a tight twist of smile. 'Is there anything else you've been keeping back which we might be interested in?'

'There is nothing else which is hidden,' I tell her, only a little disappointed with her reaction. 'Everything in the castle and the grounds is open and obvious enough. We have no weapons or medical supplies you don't know about, and you let Morgan keep her jewellery.'

She nods. 'So I did,' she says. Her smile loosens. 'Well, thank you for your contribution,' she says. 'Would you mind asking one of the men to bring the fuel round to the trucks?'

'Not at all,' I say, with a small bow, then leave and swing closed the library door, a strange feeling of both relief and exhilaration coursing through me.

This duty discharged, I climb towards you again, my dear, and stand for a moment at one of the casements in my room. The hole in the floor has been filled in and covered with both a rug and a large ceramic urn, while an old tapestry has been nailed across the ceiling and wall where the hole is. Continued thumping from above bears witness to the servants' efforts to repair the roof as best they can.

I throw open the windows to gaze through mists and scattered showers upon the far, unpopulated lands, our tent-despoiled lawns and catch – on that still veering wind, brought over the hills and across the plains – the reasserted rumble of distant artillery fire, and the smell of death's decay upon the freshening breeze.

C H A P T E R
N I N E

You are stirring, the wind is stirring a swift unmaking in the clearing air and rustling trees around us as I prepare to leave. I determine that my shoes are not sufficiently sturdy and change to a pair of stout boots, requiring a change in socks and trousers too, then of jacket, shirt and waistcoat if I am not to look ridiculous. I am careful to transfer everything from my pockets and even hang the clothes up myself.

Making my way through to your room, I find you with heavy eyes and clumsy mouth taking in a cold breakfast. I sit on your bed, watching you eat slowly. You are still breathing with some difficulty.

'Roly said', you say, wheezing, 'that Arthur is dead.'

'You shouldn't call him Roly,' I say automatically.

'Is he really?' you ask.

'Yes,' I say. You nod, continue eating.

I wonder at what I feel now and decide it is nervousness. I am used only to anticipation, not to this perhaps similar but entirely unpleasant emotion and I imagine it affects me all the more acutely because I am so unused to it. There have been scares and crises aplenty over the last few years as circumstances spiralled down – unbelievably at the time, though there is a cast of inexorability to what transpired, looking back – to the present excess of adversity, but somehow in the past I escaped this sense of dread.

Perhaps I always felt in control in the past, secure in the stewardship of our home and its distributed resources; even taking to the roads, abandoning the castle for its own sake, seemed at the time like a brave and resourceful act, finally taking our fate into our own hands when that previous resolve began to look more foolhardy than courageous. And at the end of that attempted flight, when the lieutenant brought us back, I felt concern, anger and a sort of indignant, physical fear, but all was held in check at the back of my mind by the immediacy of response our situation called for, our immersion in the demanding instant.

But this trepidation, this febrile anxiety, this apprehension of the future is something quite different. I cannot recall feeling so since I was a young child and sent to my room, to await punishment from Father.

I look around your room. Downstairs, I hear the lieutenant commanding her men, shouting out orders. The hammering continues above. The castle, surrounded, assaulted, invaded, used and pierced, holds us all; you and I, our servants, the lieutenant's men. Its old stones, still arguably inviolate, still seem now lessened; without their slighting, without the theft of any significant treasure but just by the addition of the lieutenant and her men it is brought down, reduced to something expressible in only time and matter. What for all our heritage now? Where lies the spirit of the place, and what does it matter?

For all its warlike aspect, the castle is a civilised thing, its value appreciable only in times of peace; for it thoroughly to resume its old significance and its power, all about us would have to sink even lower, to the point where no engines worked and no guns fired and people like the lieutenant and her men were reduced to arrows, bows and spears (and even then siege engines could still level it). The map the lieutenant soiled with her unwashed hair and mud-caked boots will bear less legend now, and that fine paper, representing, must support us all.

Am I doing, and have I done, the right thing? Perhaps I should have misled them over the map and somehow sent intelligence of their attack to the opposing side, then – contriving not to go with them – stayed behind and overcome whatever troops they will be leaving here in the hope that their main force is annihilated by their enemies. Perhaps I should not have told them about the fuel we hid underneath the carriage.

But still I feel I am in the right; they fight our fight for now and I pursue our own ends in helping them attempt to capture the gun. That weapon has the measure of us, and only luck prevented it from destroying half the castle – and you and I – with that first round this morning. Who knows what will happen this afternoon? My own place in any attack will perforce be at the rear, unarmed. If they fail, I should be able to run, retreat with them, or even escape their company altogether. In either event, the reason that those who fired upon the castle did so will have been removed from it and they may leave us alone. If the lieutenant's band succeeds, still surely reduced, the most immediate threat to the castle is still cancelled, brought into the lieutenant's control or simply destroyed.

And if nothing else I rid this place of them for a while. I'll lead them out of it to their own battle, and for this inconsequential episode, if no more, I will be involved; allowed to feel alive in a way I have not felt before.

Perhaps none of us will come back, my dear; perhaps only you, our few servants and the meek, damaged ones of the lieutenant's troupe will inherit the castle. I look at you, yawning, brushing a heavy fall of dark hair back from your face and spreading some butter on a ragged slice of bread, and wonder if you'll remember me fondly, or – after a while – at all.

Oh dear. I do believe this is self-pity. I am imagining myself dramatically dead, tragically taken from you and even more lamentably forgotten. What dreadful clichés war and social strife reduce us to, and how powerful the effect must be, if even I am so infected. I think I must pull myself together.

You finish your breakfast and rub your fingers, looking around for a napkin. I am reaching for my handkerchief when you shrug and use the edge of a sheet, then suck on each finger in turn. You see me looking at you and smile.

I wonder how much time we have. I ought perhaps to make the most of what may be the last occasion we see each other; pull the bedclothes from you, part my fly and quickly plant myself between your legs, urgent with the impending threat of an un-little death.

Suddenly I recall the so, so many times our love – deemed wrong, congenitally, and further enhanced by every irregularity we could devise – was made manifest within this high, wide canopied bed, this stage for our copious acts, this platform for so many provocative views: once with perfumed oils that took an age their sweet odours to remove; once with a nightdress pulled up to your neck, stretched tightly over your face, removing you in that blankness, picking out each feature of your face as you bucked and writhed (which taught me that sometimes it is the smallest twist, the tiniest, most contingent variation that can provide the greatest pleasure); indeed how many times in some way masked while at the same time naked, or with the body as disguised, by the language of dress lying about its sex; or confined, tied, with soft scarves or leather thongs, one of us made an X of between the burly posts of this great bed; or in some incontinent abasement engaged, bestial and cruel; or you, or I, leashed, our very quickness held in the power of the other – noosed, hide-strapped or with your hair when it was long, my favourite – gasping to an air-starved climax our poor looters were denied; or with others, in a tangle of candlelit and lambent bodies, smothered and abandoned within a shared blizzard of caresses, sweet and tart and gentle and fierce and lenient and strict and lubricious and raw, all slipping, struggling, pushing and forcing our way to a staggered multiplicity of release.

And, especially, that first time I shared you, towards the dawning end of a party many years ago now, before our get-togethers became quite as notorious as they later did, when, having so encouraged you, by hints, cajolings and implied example, I was allowed to find you here, unbridled upon this bed in a full plumped landscape of pure white, pinned and pinning and on a spur of pleasure jouncing, rising and falling like some abandoned vessel on a rolling, stormy swell of sea.

He was a cousin, one of my better friends and one with whom I'd rode, shot and fenced and spent many another drugged and drunken night. Now I discovered him below, harnessed and secured by tasselled satin ropes, enjoying you as you rode him, erect and arched, hands round his ankles clenched, then – once the lad had recovered from his initial surprise at my appearance and come round to the idea, and indeed, patently been further energised by the notion – for me you bowed forward, leaning to him and kissing while I joined you too, ascending and mounting close by him, parallel with his generous strokes but – tenderly, patiently, taking pains not to cause such – applying myself to a more fundamental approach. With you by a word of mine stilled, like any obedient mare, and feeling, I believe, him move beneath and within, by his efforts he realised and released in me what he sought inside both you and himself.

It was, perhaps, my finest moment. Judged by the crude technicalism and regrettably naked score-keeping that can attend such matters, we duly outdid ourselves on many a subsequent occasion, but there was a freshness, an irreplace-able, unrepeatable novelty about that first time which made it as precious – no, more precious – than the loss of virginity itself. That first act for any one of us is commonly a cause for nervousness, fumbling clumsiness and those exquisite zeniths of embarrassment only youth in full provides; it can never be attended by the physical accomplishment and the intellectual refinement of taste – the ability fully to appreciate the act that one is engaged upon – which experience only brings and which, over time, one is able to apply in subsequent variations of the deed, no matter in what specifics it may be unprecedented.

I appear to have persuaded myself. All is silent for a moment. I reach for your ankle, grabbing it beneath the covers while you look up, startled, and a door is brusquely knocked. The sound comes from my own room. We both look.

'Yes?' I say, loud enough.

'We're going now,' shouts a soldierly voice. 'The lieutenant says you've to come.'

'One minute!' I yell. I whip the bedsheets from you.

You look sullen, raising your hips to tug your nightdress up. 'Are we attempting a record?'

'Some things will not wait,' I say, minimally unbuttoning as I hoist myself towards you.

'Well, don't hurt . . .' you say petulantly.

More than pain, such unexpected forcing still takes time, however determinedly done. I bury my face between your legs, submerging in your scent, at once earthy and sea-salt tanged. I loose a lubricating mouthful of spit, then rear and take my plunge.

Another shout.

CHAPTER
TEN

A lower vestibule; in the castle's front hall, the lieutenant's opera cloak lies discarded like a velvet skin, thrown over the shoulders of a hollow armour suit standing beneath a rosette of swords upon the wall. The jeeps' engines sound cold and clattering in the courtyard. The lieutenant is talking to the soldier with the grey hair and scarred face, the one with wounds to the legs; he leans upon his makeshift crutch, dutifully taking orders. A couple of our servants stand near, watching the lieutenant, then turning their attention to me.

The lieutenant looks me down and up. 'Changed again, Abel?'

'For the better, I trust,' I say, touching my fly to ensure that all is secure again. I do not think the lieutenant registers the gesture.

The lieutenant too is dressed differently, still sporting her long boots but now, above them, tweed trousers and a waistcoat over her thick green shirt. Her camouflaged jacket and a steel helmet have to fight to re-establish the martial effect over that of the country set. The lieutenant's helmet has a green cloth cover stretched over it, and on top of that there is dark webbing, a black net stretched taut and tense and at this moment – detumescing, heart thumping – evocative.

The soldier with the scarred face mutters something to the lieutenant. She frowns, glances at the servants and bends to me, putting a hand to my arm and quietly saying, 'They'll bury old Arthur in the woods at the back; the best place might be in a shell crater – it would be deep, at least.'

I nod, surprised. 'And appropriate,' I agree. So Arthur will join Father. His ashes were scattered there by Mother, thrown to the soil of our home after he eventually returned to us, in a box, following his assassination in a foreign city.

'They'll probably cut something on a piece of wood,' she says. 'What was his last name?'

I look at her, nonplussed. 'His last name?' I say, procrastinating.

She looks at me with narrowed eyes, and I fully expect that she anticipates my ignorance. She is quite right, of course, but this is one advantage over her I cannot pass up.

'Yes,' she says. 'Arthur's last name; what was it?'

'Ignatius,' I tell her, taking the first name that comes to mind (and now I think of it, that was the name of the cousin I found you with on that night of shared occupation).

The lieutenant frowns, but then quietly transmits this false information to the scar-faced soldier, who nods and hobbles off. She smiles thinly at me and lifts her gun from its place by the wall. I had not noticed. The receptacle in which the lieutenant had placed her long gun is an old artillery shellcase our family has long used to store umbrellas, shooting sticks, canes and the like. She catches my glance as she checks her gun and shoulders it. She taps the brass cylinder with one boot. 'Smaller calibre,' she tells me, then gestures towards the door and the courtyard beyond.

'No no; after you,' I say, clicking my heels together.

Her mouth makes that little twist again, and with a nod to the two wounded soldiers in the hall, she steps outside into the light, clapping her hands, herding her charges and with a sudden urgency shouting, 'Okay! Come on! Let's go!'

I take my place in the second jeep, with her. She sits behind the driver, I in the other rear seat, with the metal machine-gun post in between us, manned by the red-haired soldier she called Karma, who for the moment is sitting down, one buttock cornered on the back of each rear seat, his feet squeezed in between our thighs.

The first jeep barks and jerks away, narrowly avoiding the stonework of the well and swinging down and out through the inner gate and across the bridge outside, over the moat. We follow it, past the well, across the damp cobbles, skidding fractionally and then dipping steeply down to the narrow gate. The engine sounds loud as we pass through the short tunnel beneath the old guardroom and between the towers. The day beyond blinds, flooding my eyes with a rich golden light. Above, the sky is cobalt.

Our lieutenant reaches into one pocket and smoothly puts on sunglasses. The driver is similarly equipped. He is helmetless but with an olive bandana tied round his blond locks; despite

133

the temperature and the skimpy protection from the elements provided by the open vehicle's windscreen, he is bare-armed, wearing a ragged T-shirt, a body warmer, what looks like some form of bullet-proof vest and, over all, a gilet, pockets heavily bulging and lapels crisscrossed with linked machine-gun rounds.

The jeep tips us back again as the arched stone bridge takes us over the moat, while the first jeep accelerates down the drive. We pass the trucks, waiting on the gravel round. Each coughs and guns its engine and comes rumbling obediently after us, exhausts clouding the sky with dark gouts of smoke. I wonder if they have already filled the vehicles' tanks with the fuel I told them of.

The lieutenant stuffs a plastic-sheeted wad of papers into my hands. Within the transparent cover I can see part of the map we looked at earlier, in the library. The lieutenant takes out a cigarette and lights it, staring ahead. The gravel of the drive sounds loud beneath our wheels. I look round as we pass by the encampment of the displaced, watched, dark-eyed, by a few drawn and anxious faces.

Behind us the two trucks trundle delicately between the close-crowded guy-ropes of the camp, their camouflage-mottled canvas-covers like a pair of swaying tents somehow made mobile amongst the rest. Beyond; the castle. Its stone blocks stand, its windows glint, the towers and battlements the clear blue sky divide, and brassy, gold, the colour of lions against the backdrop woods and sapphire sky, it endures, proud and still prevailing, despite all.

I'm leaving only to return, I tell myself. I abandon only to secure. Castles need their share of luck as well as good design; we had our allowance and more of welcome fortune this morning, when our windfall shell failed to germinate and blossom its explosive result, and I hope my stratagems

– absorbing, co-operating, watching and biding – may provide a better-thought protection than a grimly prophylactic defiance that invites only rape and rasure.

Absorb like the land, co-operate like the farmer, watch and wait like the hunter. My strategies must remain hidden beneath the appearance of things, like the geology that's only hinted at by the surface of the world. There, in the hard palatal shift of underlying stone, the real course of histories and continents is decided. Buried within the indefinite edge stressed in continual shock below and obeying their own trajectories and rules, the pent powers that shape the future world lie; an ever-blind rough gripping of darkly fluid heat and pressure, holding and withholding its own stone store of force.

And the castle, dredged from rock, fashioned from that hardness by flesh and brain and bone and by the tides of all competing interests of men, is a poem carved from that strength; a brave and comely song of stone.

I think I see you, my dear, at a high window, robed from my sight, and waving. I wonder whether to return the salute, then become aware of the lieutenant at my side, also turned round, looking back to you. She adjusts the webbing on her helmet, blows out a cloud of smoke that's whipped away on the slipstream of our progress and turns round again.

When I look back, you are gone, replaced by a glittering reflection of fiery light, set amongst those bright, honey-coloured stones like a shimmering liquid jewel. Above, the three suspended looters sway in the breeze, forsaken; and over all, with a heavy, artless grace and with no choice but to be driven by the firm, coercing wind, our old memento, our new-found emblem, the flag, waves all of us goodbye.

A moment later we round a bend within the trees, and the castle by its own grounds is denied.

CHAPTER ELEVEN

The land is warm beneath the sun's high hand, the light falls prone and further shades the seasons' pastel scatter; this road, here made golden by a recent shower, steams like a burnished causeway to the sky. We move quickly and alone, coursing through the surfaced, climbing writhes of stagy, sun-struck mist, trailing our exhausts like broken puppet strings amongst the avenues of trees. The softly steaming roads are quiet and still, if not empty; we pass ditched carts and trailers, trucks fallen on their sides or angled into culverts, wheels cocked to the air, noses stuck down into the watery troughs. More trucks, buses, vans, pick-ups and cars make chicanes of the road's long straights, their bodies burned out, or overturned or simply left. All speak of the crowds who've passed this way, discarding these metal carapaces like tender-bodied crabs on the floors of seas, moulting off their past anatomies. We weave through their lifeless desolation like a needle through a frayed tapestry of ruin.

Piles and trails of abandoned possessions further block the road, and here you see the wretchedness of the refugees' imagination, if not their lives themselves, by what they thought at first to bring, and then discard; electrical goods, cheap ornaments, potted plants, whole libraries of records, gaudy piles of magazines made sodden by the rain . . . as though in their sudden panic they seized upon what was nearest them at the time when the realisation dawned that staying put was no longer such a good idea.

There are no dead bodies I can see, but here and there are piles and trails of clothes, strewn by wind or animal across the fields and the surface of the road, sometimes by chance arranged in a rough semblance of a human shape and so attracting the startled eye. We drive straight over much of the wreckage, scattering pots and pans, lampshades, boxes and plastics casings. We bounce over the heaped, bedraggled clothes, scattering them behind.

Our driver sweeps and swerves, seemingly aiming for certain items of wreckage missed or left in the wake of the jeep in front; he whoops and laughs as he disposes of another derelict household effect or catches a pan left spinning in the front jeep's wake. His naked flesh has stippled with cold, but he does not seem to notice. His olive bandana ripples in the wind, his sunglasses glint. The lieutenant sits with one leg drawn up on the sill of the door, her long gun's stock resting on her lap beside her radio, barrel raised to the wind like a whip. The soldier in front of me sits similarly, and checks and re-checks his gun, snapping magazines out then in, out then in.

Occasionally he leans forward and, with a small rag produced from a pouch at his waist, oils a few more square millimetres of the weapon's gleaming surface. Dressed in long, laced boots, bulkily rustling fatigues and a quilted jacket that I think was once white but which has been smeared with paints impersonating every colour of mud from brown to black to red, yellow and green, he wears a metal helmet similar to the lieutenant's but with the words DEAD INSIDE scrawled on the green cloth cover, in what looks like scarlet lipstick.

Behind and above me, Karma wears a pair of plus-fours liberated from a farm topped by a fur coat from one of our wardrobes, worn over his combat jacket; the hands clutching the stirrup-handled rear of the machine-gun are cocooned in ski-gloves, one of which has had the top half of the index finger removed to allow better access to the gun's trigger. On to his metal helmet's fabric cover are sewn medal ribbons awarded to one of my ancestors.

The soldier in front of me rattles out the magazine once more. He inspects the gleaming rounds nestling inside, turns the tape-twinned clip over and repeats the process, then snicks it back into place again. I can smell the gun's oil. He starts to sing; something vaguely recognisable as popular, from several years ago. The lieutenant reaches into a satchel by her feet – something on her hand catches my eye and I think of the bag of jewels you held at your feet in the carriage – then sits back and clips a couple of hand grenades on to the front of her jacket. The grenades' square-cut faceted surfaces make them look like plump bars of dark chocolate. She lights another cigarette.

I have seen hunts not so different from this. Four-wheel

drives with air-conditioning instead of jeeps with machine-gun mounts, horse-boxes rather than trucks, shotguns, not automatics. Still we float along just so; for either set the cast is much the same. The lieutenant possesses her own style, sweeping along, sunglassed, lips clenched around a cigarette, staring forward. Her men too have their own combat chic. They inhabit odd items of sometimes inappropriate military gear – a brigadier's cap, some gold but grubby epaulets stitched on to a combat jacket, an ostentatious show of rotund black hand grenades plastered everywhere across a gilet like badges on a vest. Others sport pieces of civilian property – a gaudy waistcoat worn beneath the camouflage, another martially dubious hat that may have been a yachtsman's, a ring-pull from a drinks can worn as an earring – many worn, I suspect, as much for their assumed good-luck value as for any supposed expression of individuality.

And in some ways we are outdone. Our hunts were frivolous; mere games for those with the time, land and resource to spare for such pursuits. The lieutenant's purpose is more serious, her mission bearing an import greater than any we displayed; more than the life or death of a few feeling animals hangs in the balance now. All our fates, and the castle's, are piled together upon the scale's swung platform, awaiting a judgment delivered not by any judiciary, however partial in its view, but by naked force of arms.

These levelling times remain unfair, and commonise, demote, in such a civilised, cultivated countryside, what should be free from vulgar threat. Such sick suspense and mayhem all around, seem to me to belong in cruder climes, where less has been built up to be brought down. But therein lies our original mistake, perhaps; each inaugurating side in this could not believe we would reduce ourselves to the savagery we have embraced.

I wonder at the history of the lieutenant and her men. They seem at least semi-soldierly, for all that they are obviously irregulars, looking out only for themselves, not part of any larger force nor paying any conspicuous allegiance to a greater cause. Still, their vehicles, it occurs to me, are army, or ex-army. Most of the bands of fighters now roaming the land – little more or less than bandits – we've heard favour, or have no choice but to requisition and employ, ordinary four-wheel drives, or pick-ups. In contrast, the lieutenant's men have proper military trucks and jeeps, and their weapons seem of a piece: several heavy machine-guns, automatic rifles, rifle grenades, matching automatic pistols. I had thought they might add my shotguns and rifle to their arsenal, but if they have, such weapons are patently not their first choice. They seem, in retrospect, quite disciplined too. Were they a regular army unit, once?

I decide to ask. I look at the lieutenant, sitting, staring ahead, eyes hidden behind the black sunglasses. She turns her head briefly as we pass a road junction and a canted but still legible signpost, then looks forward again. I ponder the best way to approach. She takes out her silver cigarette case, opens it and selects one. I lean over towards her, past Karma's intruding knees. 'May I?' I ask, pointing at the case as she is about to close it.

The mask that is the sunglasses regards me; I see my own distorted reflection. Her lips twist. She holds the case out towards me. 'Sure. Help yourself.'

I take a cigarette; we bend towards each other as she lights mine, then hers. The cigarette tastes acrid and harsh; it must have dried out over a year or more ago to become so bitter. I had wondered where the lieutenant found her tobacco, surmising there might still be some link, however circuitous and unsafe, however much the preserve of smugglers and the desperate, to wherever peace and a semblance of prosperity might still prevail, but these dry tubes have surely been raided from ruined shops or taken from the fleeing dispossessed; no hint here of a fresh supply.

'I didn't know you smoked, Abel,' she says over the noise of the jeep's progress.

'The occasional cigar,' I say, trying not to cough.

'Hmm,' she says, drawing on the cigarette. 'Nervous?' she asks.

'A little,' I tell her. I smile. 'I imagine you must be inured to this sort of thing by now.'

She shakes her head. 'No. Some people get numb to it.'

She flicks ash to the wind, faces forward again. 'But they usually die soon after. For most people the first time is the worst, then it gets better for a while, if you have time to recover in between, but after that, usually soon after that, it just gets worse and worse.' She looks at me. 'You get better at hiding it, that's all.' She shrugs. 'Until you just crack up completely.' Another draw on her caustic cigarette. 'Opinion amongst us is divided on the subject of whether it is better to go a bit crazy every now and again and try to get it out of your system, though at the risk of losing it completely, or bottle it all up in the hope we are overtaken by events and peace breaks out, so we can be post-traumatically stressed in comfort.'

Grief, they have even thought this through. 'A grim choice,' I say. 'But you must have been trained for this, mustn't you?'

Her head jerks back and she makes a sound that may be a laugh. 'The army's training was a little rushed by the time most of our little band came along.'

'Were you always—?'

The radio crackles; she holds one hand up to me as she

raises the instrument to her ear. Wires trail from the base of the radio, leading under the driver's seat in front. I realise suddenly that only the vehicle's engines, and therefore fuel, keep the radios recharged and operating. I am not able hear what is transmitted, and her reply is so quick and terse I cannot make out those words either.

The lieutenant taps our driver on the shoulder and leans forward to speak in his ear; he begins to flash his lights at the jeep in front and wave one arm, while the lieutenant swivels to the rear, gesturing to the trucks behind.

We slow, the vehicles draw up by the roadside, and I am required to stand to one side, kicking stones into a waterlogged ditch while the lieutenant carries out another briefing of her men. I throw the cigarette end into the still, deep waters of the ditch; it hisses once. Beyond, whole fields are flooded, the irrigation and drainage system of the entire plain upset by the lack of human tending.

The lieutenant spreads maps over the front of a jeep, pointing and gesturing and looking in turn at her men, commanding them by name.

We resume our transport, shortly turning on to smaller roads, then taking to a steep track that leads up the side of a small valley. The lieutenant seems tense, and does not wish to talk; my attempts to revive our earlier conversation elicit only grunts and monosyllables. She smokes no more cigarettes. Our jeep takes the lead and, after someone has gone on ahead on foot, we arrive at the rear of a farm on the hillside; the lieutenant leaps out and disappears inside the farmhouse.

She reappears a few minutes later, goes to the rear of one of the trucks and is handed down a bag I recognise. It is the one I put the shotguns and my rifle in when we fled in the carriage. By the look of it, it is still as heavy. She carries it into the farmhouse. Behind me, Karma scans the hillsides and woods with a pair of binoculars, tensing to concentrate on one skyline, then relaxing. 'Scarecrow,' I hear him mutter.

The lieutenant comes back without the bag. 'Okay,' she says to the others in the jeep, reaching in to take the satchel that was at her feet.

Both trucks and one of the jeeps are parked in a tall, three-sided barn facing into the farm's courtyard. The lieutenant checks the maps with me. I point out the first part of the route from here while one of the soldiers – face painted with streaks of green, black and yellow – looks on too. A man I have not seen before – a farmer from his dress and manner – opens a stable door and leads out a dozen horses. They constitute a mixture of old and young, colts, mares and geldings. There are two that look like thoroughbreds, and a huge muscled pair with broad, hair-fringed hooves. Saddles are placed on the smaller animals; packs from the trucks are loaded on to the farm horses' broad backs.

'Hop on,' the lieutenant tells me, climbing inexpertly on to the saddle of a black mare and fumbling with the reins. She looks down at me. 'You do ride, don't you?'

I swing up and into the saddle of the chestnut gelding alongside her mount. I pat its neck and settle, ready, while she is still sorting the reins and trying to find her other stirrup.

I stroke my mount's mane. 'What's his name?' I ask the farmer.

'Jonah,' he replies, walking off.

I rather wish I had not asked.

Mr Cuts and another half-dozen soldiers clamber on to the remaining horses.

Three soldiers take the jeep not secreted in the barn and drive back down the track we arrived on. Two men are left at the farm to guard the other three vehicles. One of the lieutenant's soldiers – the one who studied the map with us – scouts ahead. He carries a small radio but no pack and is armed only with a knife and pistol. Horses to the front, we set off following him further up the hill, across a steep field and into a dense and tangled wood.

The lieutenant manages to make her nag drop back until for a moment she is level with me. 'We keep very quiet from now, all right?'

I nod. She does too, then kicks her horse ahead again.

The path narrows; branches scrape and tug and try for eyes. We have to duck, avoiding, and the heavy horses wait patiently for their caught packs to be freed. Our lessened band plods on, over a succession of jumbled dips and crests in the earth like an ocean swell made solid and fixed aslant to the hillside. The air is still and silent in the dim half-light beneath the crowding tracery of boughs and dark towers of conifers. The lieutenant takes the lead, ungainly on her black mare. I alone ride well. My mount snorts, its own breath wavering a reversal in the chilling air.

Behind us, trying to quiet their weapons' clatter and still control their nags, the lieutenant's brave brutes struggle, battling already.

Someone retches, near the back of our troop.

We stop at a fork in the track, where our scout is waiting. His fatigues and steel helmet appear to have sprouted a small forest of twigs, fir fronds and tufts of grass. The lieutenant and I consult the map, our legs touching, horses nuzzling each other. I indicate our route to her and the scout. As I point at the map, I notice that my hand is shaking. I withdraw it quickly, hoping the lieutenant has not noticed.

147

We ride on up the steep and narrow path. I think I detect the smell of death upon the air as it filters through these dank woods. In my belly something stirs, as though fear is a child that either sex may nurture within their bowels. The continual trough and rise of stunted ridges, convoluted, seem like the contours of the human brain exposed by the surgeon's knife beneath the bloody plates of skull, each surface-deep division concealing a malignant thought.

Above the thick pelts of the evergreens and beyond the fractured assemblage of black, leaf-bare branches, the sky that once was blue now seems leeched of colour, turned to the shade of wind-dried bones.

CHAPTER
TWELVE

This will not go well, something says within me. The body knows (something whispers); the ancient instincts, the part of the mind we once called heart or soul can judge such situations more shrewdly than the intellect, can sniff the air and clearly know that only evil can result from whatever's been embarked upon.

I become my own tormentor; every sense with every other fights to make the most of each sensation, and so the least of sense in all, producing a hall of clashing mirrors for nervous over-emphasis itself to ambush there. I try to calm my distraught thoughts, but the very substance of my self seems to lack all purchase. What was solidly dependable is now liquefied and draining and there is nothing to hold that does not quickly seep away, leaving behind a hollow vessel whose emptiness only magnifies every rumour of peril the scraped-raw nerves rush to report.

Around me, every shaded patch of ground becomes the lurking shape of men with guns, each bird flitting between the branches transforms itself into a grenade hurled straight at me, every animal rustling in the underbrush at the path's side is the prelude to a leap, attack, and either the hammer-blows of gunfire striking my body or a hand clamped over my eyes and a blade pulled merciless and slicing across my throat. My nose and mouth are filled with the reek of forests in decay, the scent of brutal, pitiless men lying sweating as they prepare to fire, and the odour of sleekly oiled guns, each one filled with death and swinging to us as surely as weathercocks point out the breeze. At the same time, it seems to me that our every passing noise – the horses' breath, the merest flick of slid-past leaf or snap of twig – screams with furious enunciation, broadcasting our progress and intent to the forests, plains and hills.

I close my eyes, clench my hands. I will my gut to cease its churning. One of the soldiers was sick, I tell myself. I know; I heard him just a few moments ago. Their faces have been pale all day, nobody has eaten since breakfast. Several disappeared round the back of the farm when we stopped, to void from one end or other. You must not give in. Think of the shame; to have to stop, to dismount, run for cover, drop your trousers, have them laugh at you as you squat there, forced to listen to their remarks. Think of the lieutenant's expression, her feeling of victory, of superiority over you. Do not let this be. Do not give in!

Then my horse comes to a halt.

I open my eyes. We are all stopped. The soldier sent ahead

earlier is standing by the path-side, whispering to the lieutenant. She turns back, looks down the line of mounted men. She makes some hand signals I do not follow, and two soldiers dismount, hurrying forward, past me. Both have camouflaged faces and uniforms stuck with pieces of plants. One carries a long, black crossbow. So we are already reduced to this, I think.

The lieutenant gives them orders; the three men lope on ahead.

The lieutenant holds up her arm, points at her watch and splays five fingers. I look round to see most of the others dismounting. Several disappear silently into the bushes. The men, I notice, have become more conventionally soldierly in their dress; the gaudy items of their dress, the found mementoes from the castle have all vanished to be replaced by the dull drabness of camouflage gear. The lieutenant watches them, smiling. I pat Jonah gently on the neck, then sit back, arms folded. The lieutenant turns forward again, looking on up the path where the three soldiers disappeared. Her back looks tense.

I slide quietly off my horse and pace quietly through the undergrowth downhill, aware of the lieutenant watching me. I stop by a tree and undo my fly. I stand, apparently ready, then look to my side, as though only now noticing her watching me. I regard her for a moment, then walk a little further away, behind a tall bush. I think I see her smile, before I'm hidden from her.

At last. I quickly tug my belt free, squat and release. A happy breeze above provides a gently overwhelming susurration of sound. I have chosen the right direction; the current of the air here flows away from the path. A handkerchief suffices, sacrificed.

153

I rejoin the rest, carefully buttoning my fly. The lieutenant is still intent on the path ahead. As I remount, there is some movement at the point where the lieutenant's attention seems focused. She makes another signal to the rest, and shortly we continue up the rising path.

We pass the two killed sentries a minute later. They were in a little covered trench some way off the path, uphill in the trees. They have been dragged out of their nest, loose and slack and left together on the sloping ground outside. Both are young, dressed in combat fatigues; one has a crossbow bolt through his left eye, the other has had his throat cut so deeply his head is almost severed from his body. Looking closer, the other's throat has been cut too, but more elegantly, less messily. Our two soldiers wipe their knives upon the fatigues of the men they've killed, and look proud. The lieutenant nods in appreciation and makes a signal; the bodies are bundled back inside the trench, falling slackly. Horses are led forward for our two heroes to remount; the third man, the scout, has disappeared again.

We find the gun ten minutes later. At a signal from the scout the lieutenant has us gather in a hollow and dismount. The men shoulder their heavy packs and heft their weapons; the horses are tethered to trees. The lieutenant looks over her men, eyes flitting over faces, packs, guns. She whispers to a few, smiles, pats them on the arm.

She comes to me and puts her mouth to my ear. 'This is the dangerous bit, Abel,' she whispers. 'Soon the shooting starts.' I can feel her breath on my cheek, sense the physicality of this low murmur entering the soft convolutions of cartilage and flesh. 'You can stay here with the horses, if you like,' she tells me. 'Or come on with us.'

I shift my head, put my lips to her ear. Her olive-dark skin smells of nothing at all. 'You'd trust me with the horses?' I ask, amused.

'Oh, you'd have to be tied up,' she says softly.

'Tied up or getting to watch,' I tell her. 'You spoil me. I'll come.'

'I thought you might.' Suddenly there is a huge, serrated knife in front of my eyes, its blade covered with matt stripes of dark paint, only the extremity of its scalloped edge left naked in a wavy, shining line. 'But not a sound after this, Abel,' she breathes, 'or it'll be your last.' I tear my gaze from that fearsome blade and try to detect some irony in those grey eyes, but see only the reflection of still greyer steel. My eyes have gone wide; I narrow them and smile as tolerantly as I can, but she is already turned and gone. In the distance, on the breeze, I can hear an engine running.

We leave the horses, cross a low bank and another shallow depression then clamber up the steep, root-rutted side of a taller ridge; the engine noise grows louder all the time. At the summit of the incline, in the midst of damp, brown bracken through which the lieutenant and her men insinuate themselves with delicate grace and minimal disturbance – which I attempt to emulate – we come out above a cliff.

The gun stands caught in sunlight, barely a grenade's throw away. It lies in the middle of an old mine's buildings, surrounded by the ruins of a failed enterprise; a corroded lattice of brown, narrow-gauge rails, a tilted, rickety wooden tower topped with a single wheel, peeling, tumbledown sheds with vacant, shattered windows, skewed and crumpled corrugated iron roofs and a scatter of dented, rusting drums.

The gun alone looks efficient and whole, its metal form a dull, dark green. Its body is longer than the trucks we left

155

in the farm. It rests on two tall rubber-tyred wheels; beneath the barrel there is a parallel pair of long, sealed tubes and protecting its crew there is a flat plate sloped over the breech, where a confusion of wheels, handles, levers and two small bucket-seats are perched above a broad circular base that looks as if it can be lowered to take the weapon's weight.

Behind, two long, spade-footed legs have been swivelled together to form a towing bar. A group of soldiers is engaged in hooking it up to a noisy farm tractor, while behind them an open-decked civilian truck waits, engine idling. A few other uniformed men are loading bags, packs and boxes on to the truck, making journeys from the least ruined of the mine's buildings; a two-storey brick construction that looks as if it was an office. I count only a dozen men altogether, none of them carrying obvious weapons. The smell of diesel exhaust drifts on the air.

The lieutenant, beside me, uses her field-glasses, then whispers urgently to her men; orders are passed along the line in each direction, over my head. I sense an excitement in her communicating itself to her soldiers, two groups of whom are scuttling away on either side just below the summit of the ridge, their shadows scattering, merging dark in darkness. They are moving quicker than they did on the approach, any noise they make covered by the engines and the favouring wind. The lieutenant and the remaining third of her little force are all reaching into packs, withdrawing magazines and grenades.

I look around, at the perfect, lifeless blue of the sky above, at the mass of dark fir-trees on the ochre slope behind the mine, at the orange sun, hanging on the hill's far rim like fingers clawing a ledge, then down at the gun again, now held within the shade of the western hills. It has been secured to the tractor. The truck behind is moving now, the driver leaning half out of his opened door as the vehicle backs up by the side of a fallen-down building towards a twin-axled trailer covered with a tarpaulin. Four soldiers get behind the trailer and try to shift it forward to meet the truck, but fail. They laugh, voices echoing, and shake their heads, settling for beckoning the truck onwards.

The lieutenant stiffens suddenly; she tilts her head, as though listening for something, or to something. She looks at me, frowning, but I think does not see me. Perhaps I can hear something. It might be distant gunfire; not the nebulous thudding of artillery but the flat crackling of automatic small-arms. The lieutenant steadies her gun, lowering her cheek to the stock. The soldiers lying along from her see this and take sight too.

I look back to the soldiers at the mine. The tractor sits idling, connected to the gun. They seem to be having problems with the trailer's towing point. Half a minute passes.

Then a soldier comes running out of the brick building, waving a rifle and shouting something. Instantly the mood changes; the soldiers start looking around, then move; some head for the office building, others make for the cab of the truck, where the driver is standing on the cab's step, looking, it seems, right at us.

Then firing sounds from somewhere to our right, and the ground beneath the soldiers heading for the office building leaps and flicks in miniature detonations of earth and stone. Two men drop.

The lieutenant makes a hissing noise, then her gun erupts, spearing flame and hammering twin spikes of pain into my head. I jam my fingers in my ears, eyes screwing up involuntarily, as I duck back and down. The last thing I see of the mine is the windscreen of the truck shattering white, pocked with wide black holes, and the driver being thrown back, falling and folding as though belly-kicked by a horse.

157

The firing continues for some time, punctuated by the sharp snap of grenades falling amongst the buildings of the mine; I glimpse up to see the lieutenant pausing to flip her magazine, then again to change the spent pair for another taped-together set lying by her hand, each movement executed with a smooth, unhurried skill; the gun barks on, hardly pausing. The air reeks with a bitter, acrid scent. A couple of thuds behind and below may be the impact of returned fire, and I think I hear the lieutenant's radio squawking, but she is either ignoring it or cannot hear. Soon the only sound is from the lieutenant's guns and those of her men.

Then it stops.

The silence rings. I open my eyes fully, gazing at the prone form of the lieutenant. She is looking along the row of men lying by her side. They are each looking, checking. All seem uninjured.

I pull myself back up to the little tunnel of flattened bracken I left at the summit of the cliff and gaze down to the mine. A little smoke drifts. Some of the office building's windows look eroded, the metal frames buckled, the brick surrounds edging them pulverised to curves, with flakes and fragments of orange brick scattered on the ground beneath. The front of the truck looks as though a giant has filled an immense brush with black paint and then flicked it, spattering dark spots all over the metalwork. Steam issues from its grille and the holes punched in its engine cover. A dark pool of diesel spreads slowly out from underneath like blood beneath a corpse. The tractor lists, one tall rear wheel and both front tyres flattened. Bodies lie fallen and sprawled all across the ground, a few with guns at their sides or still clutched in their hands.

Then, movement at the door of the office building. A rifle is thrown out, landing and skidding along a length of the

narrow-gauge rails. Something pale flutters in the doorway's
gloom. The lieutenant mutters something. A man hobbles out
of the building, face bloody, one arm dangling, the other
waving what looks like a sheet of white paper. He is shot
from our right, his head flicking back. He falls like a sack of
cement and lies still. The lieutenant makes a tutting noise. She
shouts something but the words are lost in the sound of firing
coming from the top storey of the office building. Returning
fire from our right flank kicks dust out from the bricks around
the window and then, with a bang, something flashes over
the tractor, gun and truck and disappears through the same
opening; the explosion follows almost immediately, pulsing a
quick cloud of debris through the window and shaking dust
from the eaves of the building's corrugated iron roof.

The silence resumes.

I stand upon the track at the entrance to the mine's compound
in the deep dusk light; the sky is a cooling turquoise bowl above
the dark, silent crowds of trees. The sunlight drains slowly up
the slope beyond, falling back before the shadows. The air is
fragrant, full of the smell of pine resin, replacing the stink of
cartridge smoke. The dull red gravel beneath my feet rasps as
I turn to survey the killing ground.

I watch the lieutenant's men as they cautiously check the
prostrate forms littering the earth, guns levelled and ready as
they frisk and search each body, expropriating guns, ammunition and whatever else takes their fancy. One of the fallen
moans as he's turned over on his back and is quieted with a
knife, breath gurgling from the wound like a sigh. Curiously
little blood.

The lieutenant has checked the gun, finding it intact; Mr
Cuts seems fascinated by it, climbing over it to test its controls,

spinning metal wheels, hauling on its levers, pulling the shining steel plug of the thread-ridged breech open and sticking his nose inside. The lieutenant tries to use the radio, but has to climb back up to the ridge before making contact. The trailer behind the truck is opened, revealing boxes full of shells and charges for the field gun.

The back of the devastated truck yields more ammunition, various supplies, food and several crates of wine, mostly undamaged.

The jeep that left the farm appears up the track, heralded by a shout from the man the lieutenant has left on the ridge. The men from the jeep all whoop and laugh and back-clap those who took the mine, telling of their own fire-fight, surprising another truck further down the track leading to the mine. Stories are told, joking insults traded, and a sense of relief fills the air, as obvious and sharp as the scent of pine. Two dozen or more they have killed. In exchange; one trivial flesh wound, already cleaned and bandaged.

Something moves at my feet. I look down and there at my feet, like another wounded soldier, I see a bee, crawling heavy and awkward, clambering blindly over the cold surface of the gravel track, dying in its thick, furry uniform as the season's chill turns against it.

Another shout from the man on the cliff-top and an engine's roar comes from down the track. One of the trucks from the farm comes bustling up, lights flashing. It rumbles straight towards me; I have to step back off the track to let it roll growling past. It turns, swaying, in the centre of the buildings and grates to a stop. I look down at where its wheels passed, expecting . . . but the bee, uncrushed, crawls on.

We leave quickly after that; the truck takes the gun, booty and us, while the jeep leads the way, struggling with the weighty ammunition trailer. At the farm the second truck assumes the burden of the trailer and the farmer is breezily informed where his horses may be found. His look is dark but he wisely holds his tongue.

The lieutenant takes to her jeep again; I am left in the rear of the second truck with some of the joking soldiers; a bottle of wine is pressed into my hand and a cigarette offered as we jolt down the track and into the gathering darkness beneath the trees.

There is one last act, just before we find the first narrow metalled road; a jolt of brakes and a burst of gunfire from ahead sends everyone diving for their guns and helmets. Then shouts tell us the matter's settled.

It had been a pick-up, full of comrades of those killed at the mine, shot even as they hailed the lights approaching them. They too are dispatched without injury to the lieutenant's men, only one of their number even escaping the bullet-torn vehicle, to die face down on the track. The pick-up, on fire, is nudged out of the way by the leading truck, settles on its side in a weed-choked ditch beneath the trees, and begins to crackle with exploding ammunition. We leave it blazing in the night alone, and bump off, singing, for the road.

I watch that distant burning for some time as we ride the long straight road back. The blazing pick-up, the bushes, the overhanging trees and whatever lies about to be infected by their fever produce a pyre that grows and yet does not; a quivering, climbing conflagration beating at the night sky and spreading just as we diminish it by moving off from it, so that the whole unsteady mass seems fixed, and that furiously unrepeatable consumption, for a while, enduring.

161

But then, from the cold jolting of the truck's open rear, swinging wildly through the bends created by empty vehicles long abandoned, I watch as all we have consigned to the starry night's attention eventually succumbs, and the glaring flames die down.

I do not sing or shout, or drink, or laugh with the merry crew I share the truck's side-benches with. Instead I wait, for an ambush, crash or climax that does not come, and when, in this night's loud midwinter, we turn into our home's drive, I sense the castle's bulk both with surprise and a sick, sure disappointment.

CHAPTER
THIRTEEN

The hand's grasp near fits the skull, the covering bone by bone enclosed. And saying this, we grasp that.

We each contain the universe inside our selves, the totality of existence encompassed by all that we have to make sense of it; a grey, ridged mushroom mass ladled into a bony bowl the size of a smallish cooking pot (the lieutenant's men should look inside the webbed and greasy darkness of their own tin helmets, and see the cosmos). In my more solipsistic moments, I have conjectured that we do not simply experience everything within that squashed sphere, but create it there too. Perhaps we think up our own destinies, and so in a sense deserve whatever happens to us, for not having had the wit to imagine something better.

So when, despite my gut-felt certainty of doom, we arrive back at the castle uncrashed, not ambushed, and find it hale and whole and everyone within it present and correct, my earlier dread vanishes like mist before the wind, and I feel a curious sense of victory, and even, contrarily, of vindication. As ever, when in this fervidly self-referential mood, I decide that whatever unsleeping force of will continually keeps my life steered to a safe and proper course has triumphed over the half-sensed vagaries of a current that might have led to danger. It could be that I have kept the lieutenant and her men safe from a disaster that would have befallen them had I not been present; perhaps I have indeed been their guide in more ways than they know.

Still, as we roar swaying up the drive, lights making a tunnel of the grey and leaf-bare trees, I consider this supposition, and consider it, to be charitable, unlikely. It is too neat, too self-contained; one of those facile faiths to which we give credit, but draw none from, and whose only certain effect is to make us become what does not become us.

The trucks draw up outside the castle, the men jump down, and laugh and shout and joke. Tailgates bang flat, rattling chains, the gun's unhitched, the plunder from the mine is manhandled, thrown down and carried off and the soldiers left in the castle rush out to meet those returned from the fray. Backs are slapped, pulled punches thrown, rough hugs exchanged, bottles are clinked and hoisted, and the raucous laughter of relief fills the night air with steaming breath.

I climb demurely down, unable to join in all this hail-fellowing. I look for you, my dear, thinking you might be with this welcoming crowd, or just watching from a window, but you do not appear. I see the lieutenant, smiling by her new-won cannon, surrounded by all this rumbustious camaraderie, looking round with close appraisal at her rowdy crew, calculation written plainly on her face. She shouts, fires her pistol in the air, and in a brief trough-silence, every face turned to her, announces a party, celebration.

Break out more wine, she commands; secure some dancing partners from the camp of dispossessed, have the servants prepare the very finest feast they can from what's in store, and charge the generator with some precious fuel to turn on all the castle's lights; tonight we all make merry!

The soldiers whoop for joy, bay at the moon, and raise gun muzzles to the skies, firing in crackling, deafening agreement, a *feu de joie* to wake the dead.

A quick conference between the lieutenant and Mr Cuts, standing by the gun and looking at the bridge across the moat, while men run from truck to castle, carrying crates between them, arms bowed out in balance, others shoulder drums of fuel and head for the stables while most – directing one truck's lights at the camp of refugees – go amongst their tents, issuing invitations, indeed insisting on the company of its women at the festivities. I hear shouts, wails and threats; some scuffles start and heads are cracked, but there are no shots. The soldiers start to return, dragging partners by the wrist; some meek, some cursing, some still struggling into clothes, some hopping on grass and gravel as they put on shoes. The faces of their forsaken men, darkly desperate, watch from the shadowed tents.

The lieutenant and her deputy are decided; an attempt will be made. The gun's unhitched from its truck and reconnected to a jeep.

The lieutenant's haul is duly hauled, taken through the iron-toothed mouth of the castle's face, pulled by the grumble-engined jeep. The lumbering artillery piece barely fits, its wheels knocking stones off the bridge's balustrade to send them splashing into the black moat, the long barrel's end grating on the underside of the passageway beneath the old guard chamber. The jeep's wheels skid on the courtyard cobbles and the gun seems stuck, but the laughing men push and heave and it scrapes through and in, to be parked beside the well in the castle's hollowed core. Its great barrel is elevated to provide more room, so that those two gaping mouths, well and gun, rough stone and rifled steel, both aim towards the night, a silent concert of ill-matched calibres.

Meanwhile the second jeep squeezes in too, pulling the ammunition trailer and surrounded by soldiers dragging pale-faced women and girls, some dressed in daytime clothes, others still in night attire.

The soldiers light torches, brandish candles, throw open rooms and chuck thick logs on fires. Outside, others secure the trucks in stables and fire the generator up, flooding the castle with electric light and leaving us all blinking in the unaccustomed glare. When they return, they bring the black, wrought-iron grid of the portcullis down and lock it. The servants not already up are pulled out of their beds, the kitchen stoves are stoked, larders raided and armfuls of bottles lugged up from cellars. The ballroom's double doors are flung open and spread wide, a collection of recordings is discovered, and soon music fills the space. The fruits of my own taste quickly prove unsuitable, however, and they find fitter strains from the servants' rooms.

The lieutenant has the tall curtains pulled over to block the light's escape and quietly instructs a few of the men to take their pleasure, by all means, but also to take turns keeping watch from the roof, lest this jamboree attract unwelcome attention from outside.

The soldiers stow their guns, grenades, take off jackets, bandoleers and bits of combat clothing. Wardrobes and rooms are raided above and a group appear on the stairs laden with clothes of ours and of our ancestors. Shifts, shirts, dresses, trousers, jackets, stoles, wraps and coats of silk, brocade, velvet, linen, leather, mink, ermine and a dozen other species' hides and furs are thrown, scrambled for, pulled on, brandished with demand and reluctantly assumed; women totter on high heels, made to wear stockings, basques and old corsets. A selection of hats appears. The soldiers and their escorts sprout plumes, feathers, helms and veils; headgear gathered from half the world dances under the lights. Some of the men strap on pieces of armour, clanking round, still trying to dance. Two of them pretend-fight with swords in the hall, laughing as the blades strike sparks from naked walls; they slash a painting, try chopping candles in half. The lieutenant shakes her head, orders them to put up their swords before they hurt themselves or others.

I make to go upstairs, to look for you, my dear, but the lieutenant, smiling, brimmed glass in hand, grabs my wrist as I mount the first step. 'Abel? Not leaving us, are you?' She wears the old opera cloak again, its scarlet interior rippling within the black as she moves.

'I thought I'd check on Morgan. I haven't seen her. She may be frightened.'

'Let me do that,' she says. 'Why don't you join the fun?' She waves the glass at the ballroom where the music thumps and bodies leap and caper.

I look, and give a small pained smile. 'Perhaps I'll join you later.'

'No.' She shakes her head. 'Definitely join it now,' she tells me. 'I know.' She reaches out as Lucius and Rolans approach, one carrying a huge tray of food, the other a smaller tray stacked with opened wine bottles. She takes one of the bottles from the tray, then shoos the servants onward to the ballroom. She shoves the bottle into my hand. 'Make yourself useful, Abel,' she says. 'Top people's glasses up. That'll be your job for tonight. Wine waiter. Think you can do that? Think that's within your capabilities? Hmm?'

She seems already drunk, though there has scarcely been time. Was she drinking in the jeep on the way back, or could it be that our brave lieutenant can't hold her drink? I look at the bottle's label, trying to discern its vintage. 'I thought being your guide today might have earned me my daily bread.'

'Normally it would have, I'm sure,' she says, going up a step above me to put one arm round my neck. 'But the guys did all the shooting and you didn't, and they don't normally get to have parties in castles. Be a good host,' she says, knocking me on the chest with her glass, spilling wine on my waistcoat. 'Oops. Sorry.' She pats at the stain, wipes it with her hand. 'It'll come out in the wash, Abel. But be a good host; be a servant for once in your life; be useful.'

'And if I refuse?'

She shrugs, frowns almost prettily. 'Oh, I'd be awfully upset.' She drinks from her glass, studying me over its rim. 'You've never seen me lose my temper, have you, Abel?'

I sigh. 'Perish the thought.' I glance up the rising spiral of stairs. 'Please tell Morgan not to worry, and I'd ask you not to force her to come down here if she doesn't want to. She can be shy with people sometimes.'

'Don't you, worry, Abel,' the lieutenant tells me, patting my shoulder. 'I'll be nice as nice.' She nods to the loud ballroom and presses me on the back. 'Off you go, now,' she says, then turns on her heel and skips upstairs.

I watch her go, then reluctantly enter the ballroom. Saturnalian, I wander amongst the revellers, topping up their glasses, emptying one bottle and taking another from the supply on a sideboard. By the state of the floor, as much is being spilled as drunk. Performing this duty, I am alternately thanked with camp extravagance, or just ignored. In any event, not everyone requires my services; some of the men clutch their own bottles and drink straight from them. Their partners are at first cajoled, persuaded and bullied into drinking their share, then gradually, swept along by the music, dance and the men's boisterous bravado, some start to relax, and dance and drink for their own enjoyment.

Next door, in the dust of the partly demolished dining-room, also damp underfoot, trays of savouries, meats and sweets are being laid out and almost as rapidly demolished. A surprising amount and variety for such short notice; I suspect the castle's supply of canned food will not last out the night.

A shout, and from beneath a dust sheet the ballroom's grand piano is revealed. A soldier drags its stool out from underneath, sits, cracks his knuckles and – as the music is turned down, then off – launches into some plodding, jangling, sentimental song. I grit my teeth, and take another pair of bottles from a refilled tray. A guitar is produced, and a woman volunteers to play. A drum, draped in regimental colours, is torn from a wall and young Rolans is persuaded to thump its well-worn skin. The band of soldier, servant, refugee plays as one might expect, inaccurate, loud and wild.

The lieutenant reappears, leading you. I cease in midpour, watching. You have dressed in a sea-blue satin ballgown, arms clad in long topaz gloves, your hair gathered up, a glittering diamond choker at your throat. The lieutenant has changed too, dressed in dinner jacket, trousers and black tie. Perhaps she could not find a top hat and stick. One of my suits, it sits a little large on her, but she does not seem to care. The music hesitates as the piano player stands to watch you two enter. The lieutenant's men hoot and yell and clap. She bows with low exaggeration, acknowledges their jeers, takes up another glass of wine, hands a second one to you, then bids us all continue.

The woman playing guitar is hauled up to dance; the band takes an extended break and the recorded music resumes. The bottles of wine are shuttled up from cellar to tray to hand and their contents sloshed into glasses and throats. The room grows warm, the music's turned up, the piles of food shrink, the soldiers lead their women into dance, some lead them off upstairs, others play like huge clumsy children, disappearing to bring back some new toy discovered elsewhere in the castle. Trays hurtle down the stairs with shrieking soldiers hanging on; an old, wood-brown globe depicting the ancient world, removed from its stand, is rolled into the ballroom and kicked about; two pikes are ripped from a wall display, cushions tied over their ends and two men take one each, sitting on serving trolleys while comrades push them up and down the Long Room, jousting, laughing, falling, smashing vases, urns, ripping up carpets and tearing down portraits.

The lieutenant dances with you, in the centre of the room. When the music pauses and she leads you to the side to take up your glasses, I approach to serve. A huge crash, followed by much laughter, sounds from somewhere above. There is a thunderous noise of something heavy rolling overhead, audible even when the music resumes.

'Your men have become vandals,' I tell the lieutenant over all the noise as I refill her glass. 'This is our home; they're wrecking it.' I glance at you, but you look unconcerned, and stare wide-eyed at the dancers capering, clapping, whirling on the floor. One soldier is drinking what smells like paraffin, spitting it out, blowing fire. Beside a window, half hidden by the curtain, a couple are copulating against the wall. Another crash from overhead. 'You ordered them to treat the castle well,' I remind the lieutenant. 'They're disobeying you.'

She looks around, grey eyes twinkling. 'The spoils of war, Abel,' she murmurs lazily. She gazes at you, then smiles at me. 'They have to be let off the lead now and again, Abel. All the men you were with today probably thought they were going to die; instead they're alive, they won, they got the prize and they didn't even lose any friends, for once. They're high on their own survival. What do you expect them to do; have a cup of tea and go early off to bed with a good book? Look at them—' She waves her glass towards the crowd. Her words are slurred. 'We have wine, women and song, Abel. And tomorrow they may die. And today they killed. Killed lots of men just like them; men who could have been them. They're drinking to their memory, too, if they only knew, or to forget them; something like that,' she says, frowning and sighing.

The soldier trying to blow fire sets his hair alight; he yells and runs and somebody tries to throw a white fur-coat on him, but misses. Another man catches the burning man and empties a bottle of wine over his head, putting the flames out. There are shouts from outside the ballroom, and the sound of something coming clattering, crashing down the spiral of stone steps, smashing halfway down and tinkling.

'I'm terribly sorry they're causing a bit of a mess,' the lieutenant says, looking from me to you. She shrugs. 'Boys will be boys.'

'So you won't do anything? You won't stop them?' I say. One man is climbing up the side of the great tapestry facing the windows. Outside, in the hall, another is trying to stand on the shoulders of a comrade and grab hold of the chandelier's lowest crystal pendant.

The lieutenant shakes her head. 'It's all only possessions, Abel. Just stuff. Nothing with a life. Just stuff. Sorry.' She takes the bottle from my hand, tops up her glass and hands it back to me. 'You'll be needing to go and fetch some wine,' she says, putting the glass back on the sideboard. She reaches for your glass, puts it aside too, then takes your hand. 'Shall we dance?' she asks you.

You go with her, led out on to the floor, made way for by the other dancing couples. The fellow climbing the tapestry slips, tearing at it, shouting out as it divides in a great long rend that splits the fabric top to bottom and sends him crashing and laughing into a trolley packed with glasses and plates beneath.

I refill glasses in the dining-room and hall, watching the treasures of the castle gradually wither and fragment around me. The rolling noise overhead and crash upon the stairs was a huge ceramic urn, two hundred years old, brought from the other side of the world by an ancestor – another spoil of war, now sundered, smashed to shards and dust and lying in a glinting series of heaps and piles of debris, spread down the bottom half of stairway like a frozen waterfall of powder and glaze.

They have started taking down some of the portraits from the wall, cutting out the heads and sticking their own reddened faces through. One tries to dance, lurching unbalanced, with a white marble statue; a shining perfect nude, a fourth Grace; they scream for joy to see him trip and lose his purchase, so that the statue falls, its snowy serenity going unprotesting with him, to hit a window ledge and shatter; head rolling

174

away, each arm breaking off. They pick the soldier up and stick the statue's marble head on a helm-less suit of armour. One stands on the chandelier's broadest rim, swaying on it in a tinkling pendulum of glittering light, making it creak at its anchor-point high above.

The once outraged maids and matrons from the camp outside now stagger and whirl, squawking inebriately, opening their unproud mouths and legs to accommodate the lieutenant's men. More men are fighting drunkenly with swords, some sober instinct in them having led them to use weapons still sheathed. In the courtyard, watched by the pinched faces of the twice dispossessed men staring through the dropped portcullis, soldiers smash a bottle of wine on the barrel of the artillery piece and christen it 'The Lieutenant's Prick'.

One of their number loses a tray-race down the stairs and is carried head-high through the opened gateway – the concerned husbands and parents outside scattered by a sky-directed shot or two – and thrown into the moat. The women are thrown into our guest-room beds; bellyfuls of wine and food are thrown up into the courtyard, toilets, vases and trays.

A remote presence at the feast, the generator hums. The lights flicker, the music swells and washes over all and the bright and dusty hall resounds, full of a vacuous, aching enjoyment.

The lieutenant dances with you, leading you. You laugh, ballgown flying out like cool blue flames or silky water frothing in insubstantial air. I stand watching, taking no part. My gaze follows you, faithful, dogged, only straying to others. The oafs come up and slap my back and shove a bottle of better spirits into my hand, bidding me drink; drink this and this, smoke this, dance now; dance with this, with her, here have a drink. They slap me, kiss me and sit me at the piano. They pour a glass of wine over me, perch a plumed helmet on my head and bid me play. I refuse. They assume it is because the recorded music is still pulsing out, and with shouts and arguments have it quieted. There. Now you can play. Play now. Play something for us. Play.

I shrug and say I cannot; it is a skill I lack.

The lieutenant appears with you on her arm, both bright, glowing with a shared, emollient elation. She clutches a bottle of brandy. You hold a scrap torn from a painting; a representation of a vase of flowers, looking dull and foolish in your hands.

'Abel, won't you play?' the lieutenant shouts, bending down to me, her flushed face sheened, flesh as reddened by the wine within as her white shirt is stained without.

I quietly repeat my excuse.

'But Morgan says you are a virtuoso!' she shouts, waving her bottle.

I look from her to you. You bear an expression I have come to recognise and which I think I fell for and was ensnared by even before I knew of it; lips articulated just so, a little parted, corners tensed and turned as if with an incipient smile, your eyes hooded, dark lids drooped, those aqueous spheres lying easy and accepting in their smooth surrounds of moisture. I look for some apology or acknowledgement in those eyes, the minutest alteration to the pitch or separation of those lips that might enunciate regret or even fellow feeling, but find nothing. I smile my saddest smile for you; you sigh and smooth your spilling hair, then look away, to regard the side of the lieutenant's head, the curve of her cheek above the tall white collar.

The lieutenant punches me on the shoulder. 'Come on, Abel; play us something! Your audience is waiting!'

176

'Obviously my modesty has been of no avail,' I murmur.

I shake a handkerchief from my pocket and as the men and women still left in the hall gather around the piano, wipe the keyboard free of scraps of food, ash and spots of wine. Some of the wine has dried on the white keys. I moisten the handkerchief with my mouth. The smoothly gleaming surface of the ivory has gone the yellow shade of old men's hair.

My audience grows impatient, shuffling and muttering. I reach into the instrument and pick a wineglass off the exposed strings and hand it to someone at my side. The men and women clustered round the piano snort and giggle. I place my hands upon the keys that are the lever-ends of tusks ripped from dead things, an elephant graveyard amongst the heart-dark columns of wood.

I begin to play an air, something light, almost flimsy, but with its own lilt and delicate poise, and moving by a natural sequentiality, an inherent and unforced progression, to a more thoughtful and bitter-sweet conclusion. A silence comes upon those gathered, something settling over their energetic desire for fun like a cloth thrown over a cavorting songbird's cage. I move my hands with studiedly careful, stroking motions, the gentle dance of my fingers upon the keys a small and beautiful ballet by itself, a hypnotic feathering of flesh-enclosed bone caressing ivory with an appearance of natural fluid grace it takes half a lifetime of study and a thousand arithmetically tedious repetitions of sterile scales to acquire.

At the point where the structure of the piece would by its own implicit grammar lead to a sweetly beautiful solemnising of the main theme and a gentle resolution of the whole, I change it all completely. My hands have been a pair of gentle wings flowing over each individuated particle of air above the bed of keys, solemn and sweet. Now they become lumpen

177

talons, great arched locked paws with which I thump the pavement of the keyboard in a fatuous, one-two, one-two, one-two marching step. At the same time the melody – in its form still identifiably related to the elegantly limber figure of before – becomes a brainless, mechanical automaton of jangling discords and crudely linked harmonies crashing and lurching through the tune, and whose lumberings, in echoing that earlier beauty and reminding the ear of its dulcet fitness, mock it more flagrantly and insult the listener more thoroughly than a total change of strain and beat could ever have.

A few of my audience are so far down the road of tasteless-ness they just gawk and grin and nod along, puppets to the strings I play. More, though, stand back a little, or glare at me, make tutting noises and shake their heads. The lieutenant just reaches out and puts her hand to the keyboard lid; I get my fingers out of the way before it comes thudding down.

I turn to her, swivelling on the stool. 'I thought you'd like that,' I tell her, my voice and eyebrows raised in a tone and picture of innocence. The lieutenant reaches quickly out and slaps me. Quite hard, it has to be said, though it's done with a sort of passionless authority, as an able parent of a large brood might strike their eldest, to keep the rest in line. The noise stills the assembly even more effectively than my attempt at musicality.

My cheek tingles. I blink. I put my hand to my cheek, where there is a little blood. Drawn, I'd imagine, by the ring of white gold and ruby on the lieutenant's hand. She gazes levelly at me. I look at you. You appear mildly surprised. Somebody grabs my shoulders from behind and a draught of fetid breath washes over my face. Another hand grips my hair and my head is pulled back; the fellow growls. I try to keep my gaze fastened on the lieutenant. She holds up her hand, looking at the men behind me. She shakes her head. 'No, leave him.' She looks at me. 'That was a shame, Abel; to spoil such a pretty tune.'

'You really think so? I thought it an improvement. It's just a tune, after all. Nothing with a life.'

She laughs, throwing her head back. Gold glitters at the back of her jaws. 'Well, right, Abe,' she says. She waves the wine bottle at the keys. 'Play on, then. Play whatever you want. It's our party but it's your piano. You decide. No; a waltz. Play a waltz. Morgan and I will dance. Can you play a waltz, Abe?'

I watch you, my dear. You blink. I try to find a glimmer of understanding in your eyes. Eventually I give a small bow. 'A waltz.' I stand, open the piano stool and leaf through the sheet music inside. 'Here we are.' I open the lid and put the music on its stand. I play the music, following the stated notes. I read, play, and add the occasional pedestrian embellishment, a mere conduit for the marks on the paper, the sounds in the head of the composer, the form of the work; an excuse to hold, a soundtrack to flirtatiousness, courting, mating and fortune finding.

When I am finished I look round, but you and the lieutenant are gone. All the soldiers and their swaying conquests applaud, then the men converge on me, pin me down, tie my hands and feet with the embroidered lengths of bell-pulls and stick the helmet from a suit of armour upon my head. My breathing sounds loud, enclosed within the helm; I can smell my own breath and sweat and the metallic tang of the armour's antiquity. The view outside is reduced to a series of tiny portholes, single perforations through the ancient steel. My head clangs against the metal inside as they bear me up and carry me, trussed, outside into the courtyard where – as I am tipped and rolled about and the view gyrates wildly – the gun glints in the light of arc and flame and the cobblestones

179

glisten. They open the black iron grating over the mouth of the well, pull up the well's bucket, rattling chains, balance the bucket on the rough stone rim then set me in it, legs folded in so that the lip of the bucket digs into my spine and my knees are at my chin. Then, laughing, they push me out over the hole, hold me on the rope then let me drop. I go light; the chain rattles and the wind whistles.

The impact knocks the world away, slamming my head back against the wall then cracking it forward again, first igniting a line of fire across my back and then thrusting a spear of pain through my nose.

I sit, stunned, as the water gurgles in around me.

CHAPTER
FOURTEEN

I am dimly aware of pain and cold and the taste of metal.
Grazed, dazed, trying to shake my head, I sit here in my little wooden throne, perched within the muddy remnant of the hole's departed water, poised on a hidden platform of rubble that's choked this ornament for a century or more, still wearing my metal crown and dressed in the torn robes of a lowly calling. Water seeps in around me, beneath me, icy and and sapping.

I look up, sight constrained by my iron mask.

I was here once before, much younger. A child. Trying to see beyond the sky.

*   *   *

I had read somewhere that from a sufficiently deep hole, one could see the stars, if the day were clear. You were there, brought on a rare visit. I had persuaded you to help me with my scheme; you watched, eyes wide, fist to mouth, as I winched up the bucket, steadied it on the wall and then climbed in. I told you to let me down. The descent then was scarcely less violent than that the lieutenant's men subjected me to. I had not thought to allow for the bucket's much increased weight, your lack of strength or propensity for just standing back and letting what would happen, happen. You held the handle, taking some of the strain as I pushed the bucket off the side of the well's stone surround. Freed of the wall's support I plunged immediately. You gave a little shriek and made one attempt to brake the handle, letting it jerk and lift you on to your tiptoes, then you let it go.

I fell into the well. I cracked my head. I saw stars.

It did not occur to me then that I had succeeded, in a sense, in my plan. What I saw were lights, strange, inchoate and bizarre. It was only later that I connected the visual symptoms of that fall and impact with the stylised stars and planets I was used to seeing drawn in a cartoon panel whenever a comic character suffered a similar whack. At the time I was at first just dazed, then frightened I was going to drown, then relieved that the water beneath the bucket was so shallow, then finally both angry at you for letting me fall and afraid of what Mother would say.

High above, you looked over the edge of the well, a silhouette. So outlined, I could see you carefully holding your hair out of contact with the stone wall and the bucket's rope. You called down, asking if I was all right.

I filled my lungs and opened my mouth to speak, to shout, and then you called again, a note of rising panic in your voice, and with those words stopped mine in my throat. I sat there, thinking for a moment, then slowly slumped back, lying sprawled in the bucket, saying nothing but closing my eyes and opening my mouth slackly.

You called once more, your voice full of fear. I lay still, eyelids cracked enough to watch you through the foliage of lashes. You disappeared, calling out for help.

I waited a moment, then scrambled to my feet, pulling down on the chain until it became rope and exhausted the supply at the wooden cylinder attached to the handle on the well-head. My skull seemed to buzz but I felt unharmed. I pulled on the rope and stuck my feet out to gain purchase on the grimy stones of the well's throat. I was young and strong, the rope was new and the well only as deep as the moat's level was from the courtyard. I quickly hauled and pushed my way to the top, then pulled myself over the edge and landed on the courtyard cobbles, I could hear raised, alarmed voices coming from the castle's main door. I ran the opposite way, down to the passage under the old guard chamber leading to the moat bridge, and hid in the shadows there.

Mother and Father both appeared along with you and old Arthur; Mother shrieked, flapping her hands. Father shouted down and told Arthur to haul on the winch handle. My mother walked round and round with her hands to her mouth, circling the well. You stood back, looking pale and shocked, gulping and wheezing for breath, watching.

'Abel! Abel!' Father shouted. Arthur laboured at the winch handle, perspiring. The rope creaked on its drum, taking some weight at last. 'Damn, I can't see . . .'

'This is her fault, hers!' Mother wailed, pointing at you. You looked at her blankly and played with the hem of your dress.

'Don't be stupid!' Father told her. 'It's your responsibility; why isn't the well-cover locked?'

A terrific thrill ran through me then; I experienced a sensation I would only later be able to identify as something close to sexual, orgasmic, as I watched on while others fretted, laboured, panicked and performed for me. My bladder threatened to embarrass me and I had to clench my stomach around a ball of joy at the same time as I crossed my legs and pinched my still hairless manhood to prevent a further wetting of my pants.

Some other servants and Father's mistress appeared, crowding around the well as Arthur brought the empty bucket to the surface. My mother's wails filled the courtyard. 'A torch!' my father shouted. 'Fetch me a torch!' A servant ran back into the castle. The bucket was perched on the wall, dripping. Father tested the rope. 'Someone may have to go down there,' he declared. 'Who's the lightest?'

I was bowed in the shadows, still trying not to wet myself. A fire of fierce elation filled me, threatening to burst.

Then I saw the line of drips I'd left, from well to where I now stood. I looked in horror at the spots, dark coins of dirty well water fallen from my soaking clothes on to the dry grey cobbles; two or three for every pace or so. At my feet, in the darkness, the water had formed a little pool. I looked back into the courtyard, to where an even greater crowd had assembled, almost obscuring Father, who was now shining a flashlight down into the well and instructing servants to hold up jackets over his head so that the day's brightness would not dazzle him while he peered into the gloom.

The drops I had left shone in the sunlight. I could not believe that nobody had seen them. Mother was screaming hysterically now; a sharp, jarring noise that I had never heard from her or from anyone else before. It shook my soul, suffused my conscience. What was I to do? I had had my revenge on you – though you'd seemed only a little worried, I'd noticed – and you had already been partially blamed, but where did I go from here? This had quickly become more serious than I'd anticipated, escalating with dizzying rapidity from a great prank born of a brilliant brainwave to something that – I could tell, just from the number and seniority of adults losing their composure – would not be put to rest without some serious, painful and lasting punishment being inflicted on somebody, almost certainly myself. I cursed myself for not thinking this through. From crafty plan, to downfall, to wheeze, to calamity; all in a few minutes.

The plan came to me like a lifebelt to a drowning man. I gathered all my courage and left my hiding place in the passageway shadows, coming staggering out and blinking. I cried out faintly, one hand to my brow, then yelled out a little louder when my first cry went unheeded. Somebody turned, then all did; shouts and exclamations went up. I stumbled on a little further as people rushed towards me, then collapsed dramatically on the cobbles just before they got to me.

Sitting up, comforted, my head in my weeping mother's bosom, my hands held and rubbed by separate servants, I went 'Phew' and said 'Oh dear' and smiled bravely and claimed that I had found a secret tunnel from the bottom of the well to the moat, and crawled and swum along it until I got out, climbed up the bridge and tottered, exhausted, through the passageway.

To this day I think I was almost getting away with it until Father appeared squatting in front of me, his expression dark, his eyes stony. He had me repeat my story. I did so, hesitating, no longer quite so sure of myself. Had I said I'd climbed out via the bank? I meant the bridge. His eyes narrowed. Thinking I was plugging a gap, in fact only adding another log to my pyre, I said that the secret passage had fallen in after me; there wouldn't be any point in, say, sending somebody down to look for it. In fact the whole well was dangerous. I'd barely escaped with my life.

Looking into my father's eyes was like looking into a dark tunnel with no stars at the end. It was as though he was seeing me for the first time, and as though I was looking down a secret passage through time, to an adult perspective, to the way the world and cocky, lying children's stories would look to me when I was his age.

My words died in my throat.

He reached out and slapped me, hard, across the face. 'Don't be ridiculous, boy,' he said, investing more contempt in those few words than I'd have thought a whole language capable of conveying. He rose smoothly to his feet and walked away.

Mother wailed, screaming incoherently at him. Servants looked confused, some gazing at me with troubled expressions, some looking after him as he walked back into the castle. His mistress followed, taking you by the hand.

Arthur, whom I thought old then but who was not really, looked down from the space in the crowd Father's exit had created, his expression regretful and troubled, shaking his head or looking like he wanted to, not because I had had a terrifying adventure and then been unjustly disbelieved and harshly struck by my own father, but because he too could see through my forlorn and hapless lie, and worried for the soul, the character, the future moral standing of any child so shameless – and so incompetent – in its too easily resorted-to lying. In that pity was a rebuke as severe and wounding as that my father had administered with his twin handfuls of fingers and words, and in as much that it confirmed that this was the mature judgement of my actions and my father's, not some aberration I might be able to discount or ignore, it affected me even more profoundly.

I began to cry. And began to cry not with the shallow, hot and easy tears of childish frustration and rage, but with my first real adult anguish, with a grief by myself deflowered of petty childhood concern; great sobbing heartfelt tears of sorrow – not now just selfishly for my own narrow sense of advantage or annoyance, because I'd been found out or because I knew some protracted punishment probably awaited, though there was that too – but for my father's lost belief and pride in his only son.

That was what racked me, spread upon the castle's stones; that was what gripped me like a cold fist inside and squeezed those cold and bitter tears of grief from me and could not be comforted by Mother's soothing strokes and gentle pats and soft cooings.

Later, Mother still declared that she believed my story, though I suspect that she only said so to deny my father his last convert, to frustrate his will; another spurious victory in the decades-long campaign they waged against each other, at first mutually besieging and betraying in the castle, later apart. She agreed I needed to be punished, though to save face she asserted it was for going down the well in the first place. (My claim that I'd fallen somehow, that even my original descent had all been an accident had been contradicted by you, my dear, revealing an unfortunate respect for the truth.)

And so I was sent to my room for the first night of many, with nothing but school books for company and a prisoner's rations.

My exile brought one incalculable benefit, one utterly unlooked for bonus which would, years later, maturing, be consolidated.

You came to my room, having persuaded a servant to let you in with a pass key, so that you might apologise for what you said was your part in my offence. You brought a little pink cake you'd taken from the kitchens and hidden in your dress. You knelt by my bed. A single bedside lamp lit my tear-swollen cheeks and your wide, dark eyes. You handed me the small cake two-handed, with a near comical reverence. I took it and nodded, eating half of it in one munching gulp, then popping the rest into my mouth.

You stood up then with a strange gracefulness and lifted your dress to expose flesh from sock-top to navel. I stared, mouth stopped with a sugary pink pulp. You tucked your dresshems under your chin, then reached under my bedclothes and took my nearer hand, guiding it gently to the downy cleft between your legs, and held it there, pressing and softly rubbing back and forth. Your other hand closed around my genitals, then began to pull and stroke my sex. Moistened, encouraged, my fingers slipped into you, startling me both with that upward swallowing and with the heat discovered. I too swallowed, the pink mouthful of cake reflexively gulped.

You kneaded both of us, then, while I lay, still amazed, paralysed by the novelty of what was happening, by this next latest and most bizarre reversal of fortune. I was afraid to react, hesitant to will any action at all lest whatever astounding (and so surely of necessity precarious) combination of circumstances had brought this unexpected rhapsody about be upset by the smallest contrary deed of mine.

Guiding my engulfed fingers with a quicker, stronger beat, you shuddered suddenly, sighed, and in a moment, withdrew my hand and patted my wrist. You let your dress down, pulled the covers back, then knelt and took me in your mouth, sucking and bobbing, hair tickling my thighs.

I simply stared. Perhaps it was just that surprise, maybe – more likely – it was simply that I was still too young. In any event, there was, on that dry run, no climactic surge of joy and no issue either in the time we had. The tickling, bobbing, sucking went on for a little while until the servant, grown nervous of being discovered, knocked at the door and cracked it to mutter a warning. Letting it plop out of your mouth like a glistening lollipop, you kissed my own pink swelling, then covered it and walked with calm daintiness away; the door opened and closed for you and I was left alone.

Or not quite; I unrolled the bedclothes again to gaze upon my new but now slowly waning friend. I plucked experimentally at it as I sniffed my curiously scented fingers, but my manhood went down simply of its own accord, and I would not fully see its like again until that day the wind and rain ambushed me in the muddy woods.

You, my dear, would not witness the spectre you'd raised for a second time until our tryst on the castle's roof, a decade later, one warm night, above a party.

CHAPTER
FIFTEEN

The well's black water stinks; a soil-sweat perfume that for all its rankness seems as though it should at least be warm and enveloping, but instead is cold and sharp. I catch a hint of human odour, too, indicating that wine and food, vomited up to fall down here, have mingled with urine to create still more pungent tones to accompany the hole's own earthy scent.

I sniff back blood from my nose; the noise is loud inside the closed metal helm. I try to rise but feel paralysed by cold. I wonder how long I have lain here. I tip my head, clanging the helmet against the side of the shaft as I try to see the summit of the well. Light. Light through the perforations of the helmet, perhaps. Or not. I blink, and the view swims. My neck aches. I lower my head and still see the lights.

Seeing stars again, I lie back in the castle's gutted heart, its night-braided reaches holding me encupped, its stealing coldness infecting me, and feel myself part of its choking debris; another scattered mote, cast first to the quicker elements and then the ground, rolled along a course, a road, a bed I have no choice in determining, nor any way of leaving.

I am cells; no more, I think. This present assemblage – bones, flesh and blood – is more complicated than most such gatherings to be found on the world's rude surface, and my quorum of sense-holding plasm may be greater than other animals can muster, but the principle's the same, and all our extra wisdom does is let us know the truth of our own insignificance more fully. My body, my whole dazed being, seems like little more than a pile of autumn leaves, blown and bunched by a swirling wind and trapped, corralled by a chance of ancillary geography into a localised drift. Of what greater consequence am I than that temporary heap of leaves, that collection of cells, collectively dead or dying? How much more do any of us signify?

Yet still we do ascribe a greater pain and joy and weight of import to ourselves than to any mere clump of matter, and feel it too. We seduce ourselves with our own images, perhaps. The leaf dryly tumbling along the road is not really like a refugee.

We carry the silt of our own memories within us, like the castle's loft-stored treasures, and we are top-heavy with it. But ours is geological in its profundity, reaching back through our shared histories, blood-lines and ancestries to the first farmers, the first hunting band, the first shared cave or nested tree. By our wit we look further back, and out, so that we bear the buried stripes of all our planet's earlier geology in the strata of our brains, and contain within our bodies the particular knowledge of the explosion of suns that lived and died before our own came into being.

The deeper silt implies the grander flow, and I cannot fully join the rubble underneath, not while I breathe and think and feel. My bones could lie here comfortably enough – just minerals, cold things, 'stuff' – but not the man who thinks of this eventuality.

From this sunk hole I once thought to see the depths of heaven, to look into the past that is the ancient light of stars, and just so now, lowered to a heightened understanding, by my tormentors aided, I think I see the way into the future. From here, with this new perspective, I believe I view the castle whole, its plan spread out above me, transparent and confirmed, the earth made unopaque, revealing the building's stones raised from the land into the commerce of the rain and air.

Here is the house militant, a blocked-in enterprise huddled round a private, guarded void, its banners and its flags flown flagrant to the vulgar, following winds; a mailed fist prevailing against all levelling air.

Seminal, germinal, I lie there; something mud-bound, land-bound, evolving, and quite undismayed both by the burden of the abysmal past compressed beneath and by the columnar weight of atmosphere above bearing down, each together squeezing me, forcing me, tributary, to a greater, crasser surface.

But now is now, now is demand, and I must act.

I try to shrug or scrape the helmet off, but fail. I decide to free my hands first.

I struggle, numb with cold, attempting to undo myself. I bend my fingers and try to find purchase on the tied length of rough-textured bell-pull securing my hands. I tug and haul and wriggle my wrists inside their bindings.

A noise, above.

I look up into darkness, and am pissed upon; the urine patters down upon me, softly clanging off the helmet and hissing into the water. It is barely warm, cooled almost to the same chill as the well's still water by its passage down the cold air of the well's throat. Some shouts, and then, with a start that has my elbows jerk in beside my body, something solid hits the helmet and splashes into the water. Laughter, above; more shouts, fading then returning. Then the sound of retching.

Sickness, this time. It feels warmer than the urine. Its acrid stench rises up around me. Mostly wine, I think. More laughter, and then silence.

I continue to struggle with the bonds round my wrist. I think that if I could only see properly, even in the near darkness, I might succeed. But I need my hands to release me from the helm. I try, instead, to stand inside my little bucket, thinking that I might be able to nudge the helmet off once I can better wedge it against the side of the well. That fails too, my legs refusing to work.

I set back to work on my bonds. They have become wet and slick; my fingers slip on their greasy surface. Finally, I feel something come loose on the outside of the knot, but twist my wrists and reach with straining fingers as I might, I cannot pull on it.

I flop back, exhausted, lights in front of my eyes again. I think I miss out on a little time again.

No time passes, or some does.

I lean forward to jam the face-plate of the armour helmet against the winch's chain, then, a link's length at a time, I nudge the face-plate up until I can nod my head back, flicking the metal cover over and open. It swings and clicks. I can see at last, even if there is not much to be seen. Would that the air were fresher. I look up; a stone corona of reflected light stares back, empty.

Seeing does not help me undo the length of bell-pull. After another panting hiatus and more dizziness, I lean back, hold my tied wrists above me and reach up and forward with my mouth, angling the loose length of bell-pull towards my teeth.

The smell is appalling; moisture drips on to my face. I gag, and have to stop. When the moment and the urge both pass, I make the attempt again. Eventually I snag the loose piece and grip it with my teeth. I pull on it, twisting my wrists again and trying to force my hands through.

Something gives. My wrists are coming free. One hand slips out, wet and slippy and raw as birth. I spit the filthy rag from my mouth. I tear the grubby loop off the other wrist, then reach, arms and back protesting, and lift the weight of the helmet off my head. I let it fall into the water at my side, then try to push myself upright, hands pressing down on the bucket's rim. No success. My back aches as though fresh burned. I reach up to the bucket's chain and reel it towards me, hand over hand until that linking strand's at its fullest stretch, brought down in a series of squeaking lengths until it goes taut. I grasp it and haul and finally my wedged-in back and shins pull free.

The water is only up to mid-calf level. I try to stand but cannot; my legs buckle and I have to reach out to either side for support, leaning precariously back. Finally I push the bucket over on to its side and sit on it, waiting, shivering, for some sort of feeling to return to my legs.

I black out again, coming to sprawled in the cold, fetid water, floundering and spluttering. I kneel in its scum-surfaced chill and feel around for the bucket. I sit on it.

I do not know how much time passes. I sit with my head in my hands, trying to breathe life back into my body, shivering every now and again. At some point the background noise changes, something ends, and when I look up, sensing another alteration, full night has now resumed; the rim of rock-reflected electric light has gone and there is no halo above me any more. I put my head down, then try standing. Pins and needles assault my legs, from groin to toe. I stand there, looking up into the darkness.

It is some time before I feel ready to make my attempt. I don't know how long. Nobody else comes to relieve themselves down my oubliette, or laugh at me, and indeed it seems perfectly silent and quite dark above.

I grasp the bucket's rope again, swinging my weight on it to test it. It creaks at the top and gives a little. It feels unsafe. I am not sure I have the strength to pull my way to the top. Perhaps I should just sit here on the bucket until the morning. They will take pity on me eventually, or just remember me, and perhaps lower a rope to let me out. Or not; perhaps they will leave me here until I die, or throw rocks and stones down, burying me. Can I rely on the compassion of the lieutenant? Or on your love? I'm sure of neither.

Then I lean back, my shoulder-blades against the wall behind, and shuffle my feet forward through the water, past the bucket and the submerged helmet to the far wall of sharply curved stone. I tense and strain, levering myself up. The back of my head and my spine compete for which can produce the most anguished complaint, but I ignore them both; the chain end of the rope coils in my lap. My feet are now half a metre above water; my head is a metre above them. I rest there, wedged. I was too small to do this, that last time I was here. Like this, though, I can stop and rest on my way up the shaft, relieving my arms if they become too weakened by the effort.

I set off, pulling on the rope, my breath panting, my heart racing the higher I go. My arms start to quake and quiver and burn with fatigue; I stop to rest, arms splayed downwards and to each side, grimacing as my head and back encounter rough protrusions in the stone. My legs start to quiver too. I resume and shuffle on upwards, settling into a racked, unsteady rhythm; one hand gripping the rope, pulling, then one foot up, then the other hand, and the other foot.

I slip, near the top. One tired hand encounters something slick and slimy on that filament and my grasp fails; I jerk down, instinct clamping both hands to the rope as the winch housing creaks loudly above. My grip catches on the quick friction and I stop, legs dangling. My palms and fingers burn as if charred, making me moan into the rope as I hang there, bright stars of light flashing dizzyingly across my field of vision. I swing like a hanged man, feet bumping into the shaft's walls. Tears course down my cheeks. I push out with my feet to wedge myself. I could drop, give up, stop the pain flooding from my hands just by surrendering to the earth's seductive pull; death or unconsciousness, it scarcely matters. But something in me will not let go and knows the union of those burned hands on that cold and run-out rope for what it is; a fuse.

Moving my fingers, making them open and close on that rough surface, makes me gasp. I weep with the pain and effort; my arms are shaking so hard I am certain they must buckle and give with the very next exertion. Deciding to rest, I push up with my shoulders and almost cry out when my head drops back, unsupported, and hits off horizontal stone.

I have achieved the ground's summit; I am surfaced. I can feel and hear the difference and smell the fresher, cooler air.

I bring my feet up and out, then roll to one side, clutching at the rocky wall, almost falling back down again as my clawing grip on the stones slips. Instead I flop off the stone circle and fall down on to the cobbles of the courtyard, at the side of the lieutenant's gun, bulking in the courtyard's stony ring of darkness. I press my hands to the cold, soothing cobbles, letting the castle cool my rope-scorched skin.

The castle is not quite dark; its electric lights are out but a few old garden torches flicker, feudal. A scrappy silence reigns; I hear a distant cough, and a cry; perhaps human. I stand, waiting, breathing hard, swaying a little. The night sky sends down a little drizzle, sprinkling rain upon my upturned face; I raise my hands to its coolness, as though in surrender. The fading light of the guttering torches catches on the metal-solid mass of the gun, its dumb mouth raised to the blackness. I stumble to the nearest jeep, just to sit. I hold my hands in front of my face, flexing them despite the pain.

Sitting back, I find a bag stuffed down between the seats, and something hard within. I reach in, sucking on the pain, and bring out an automatic handgun, heavy and dully gleaming. I turn it over. Its coolness soothes my hand. I hold on to it and push myself away from the jeep, walking down to where the dropped portcullis blocks the passageway under the guard chamber. Beyond the short, dark tunnel there is a hint of firelight illuminating the broken balustrade of the moat bridge. I peer through the black grid of wrought iron.

I hear a snore, almost underneath me, from just the other side of the portcullis. I start back. There come the sounds of someone waking, shifting and muttering. I gain the impression of darkness moving, of people rising to fill the space in front of me. Then a rasp, and a match flares. I shield my eyes,

202

and through the separating grid of metal see first a hand, then a dark face, then three more. The men from the camp stare back through the pierced gate, its apertures graphing a resigned concern on to their drawn and grimy faces.

'Who is that?' I ask. The match flickers. I can read nothing in these faces; are they frightened, resigned, angry? I cannot tell. 'Do I know you?' I ask them. 'Do I know any of you? Who are you? What's happened? What time is it?'

The match flickers, near its end. Dropped at the last moment, it falls, but extinguishes before it hits the cobbles of the passageway. I open my mouth to repeat my questions, but there seems no point. I can hear shuffling, settling noises, and sense the men lowering themselves again, lying down once more.

I try the iron wheel which raises and lowers the portcullis, but the padlock has been secured. I start to turn away, then recall the key I took from Arthur's bedside and slipped into one pocket. Did I remember to transfer it when I changed my clothes? I gently pat my pockets with my free hand. I find the key, lift it out with clumsy fingers and try it, but it rattles loose in the padlock's opening, useless. The men stir at the noise, then settle back, and soon soft snores begin again.

I stand there, heavy-handed, clutching a wrong key in the almost total darkness, then turn and leave the men waiting beyond that locked but open gate and walk back up towards the heart of the castle, motive and yet motiveless, but already, I think, guessing that I am heading for some slight undoing.

CHAPTER
SIXTEEN

D ark on dark the castle stands, held in suspension in the air's warped symmetry, of some solution no guarantee, but letting me, soiled and unearthed, enter it by its unlocked door. In the lower hall, lit by a last few fitful stumps of candles, something like a massacre is tableau'd. Bodies, littered, lie; wine pools, dark as blood. Only a snort and something muttered deep in sleep witnesses that the scene is one of torpor rather than murder.

I climb the helix stairs. My feet stick on some steps and crunch on others, for all my care. In the passageways and rooms above, a welter of wrecked tables, fragmented seats and fallen desks confronts me; here are curtains, crumpled

207

in heaps beneath windows, here a dull glinting of shards and metal hoops where the chandelier has fallen and smashed; in the ballroom's fireplace the kindled remains of splintered chairs and drawers smoulder, lifting lazy curls of smoke into the gaping darkness above. Two sleeping bodies lie wrapped in the ripped remains of the wall-wide tapestry; an exposed, soldierly hand still clutches a wine bottle's neck.

Everywhere glitters the jagged wreckage of vases, lights and figurines, the spikes and blades discovered from their earlier, unshattered selves sparkling like embedded icicles in a scatter of twisted, torn scraps that were once parts of books and maps, paintings and prints, clothes and photographs, all strewn like grey and drifted snow across a landscape of deeper destruction, the resultant softness of that peaceful coating like an atonement for the violence required for its creation.

Such wanton destruction. My home, our home, laid waste, sacked and ruined; the collected treasure of a handful of centuries, an entire family tree of ancestors and half the countries of the world all obliterated in one night of frenzied abandon. I gaze around, shaking my head, my senses reeling at the realisation of the scope and scale of what has been lost here. So much beauty, so much elegance, such grace; all devastated. So many lovingly accumulated belongings, so many precious possessions, so much crafted wealth, all obliterated for an adult exaggeration of a childish tantrum; liquidated to the transitory currency of destructive glee, surrendered for no more than the fleeting, blood-hot rush the vandal feels.

There is, nevertheless, a part of me that exults in what's been done, and which feels freed, liberated by all this havoc.

Where has so much of our irregular enjoyment originated, if not from breakage? We have broken taboos and laws and moral strictures, and been the evangelically infective cause of the same behaviour in others. So much that society values and makes most of, we have slighted, exploded and broken down. The more abhorrent the act, the more we have luxuriated in it, the elemental pleasure of the deed magnified and multiplied by the delicious joy of knowing the apoplectic rage so many others would exhibit should they gain knowledge of what we've done, let alone – another wicked, erotically arousing thought – what sclerotic heights of outrage they'd achieve if they were actually to witness such an act's commission.

So much have we done with the body – our own and others – that by now there are no prohibitions left to ignore, no sanctity still to defile or sanctions remaining to be broken. We have stopped at unfeigned rape, unwilling torture and actual murder, but acted out these all, embraced great pains and courted death through sweet constriction many times. What is left that does not necessitate coercion, and thus demand that we reduce ourselves to the level of the common rapist or the menial torturer, that miserable breed who can only achieve their purpose through the material overpowering of others? Nothing, I'd thought until now.

I had believed that all that remained was the prospect of the same acts performed with a new cast and the odd, trivial variation. It was, admittedly, a matter for only a modicum of regret, something easy enough to live with, like the realisation that it is impossible to conquer every longed-for object of desire, or the distant prospect of death in old age. Now I see there was always this; the destruction of what we valued, of the property we held dear. I feel that I was blind, not to have understood that some of the morality we shared with others involved restrictions worth the breaking, and hiding in that subversion a deal of previously unglimpsed pleasure.

I do not think this is something I could have done; nostalgia, some dreg of familial feeling, respect for craft or the comprehension of the impossibility of undoing such ruination would have stopped me, but the deed having been done by others, why should I not relish it and glory in the result? Who else should? Who else deserves to? Not these casual destroyers, these temporary occupiers; I doubt they knew that the paintings they slashed to shreds, or the vase they threw against a wall or the book they tossed into the moat or the desk they smashed and burned in the grate were each worth more than they might ever expect to earn, in peacetime or in war. Only I can justly and with due discrimination appreciate what has been destroyed here. And did these materials, this wealth of merchandise and art not owe me one last balance of enjoyment, one last cherishing, even if it was just the valedictory recognition of their lost worth?

Gone, then. And with all that, vanished too is so much of what drew us back even as we left the castle, those few days ago. We may now relinquish these walls unencumbered, I think. Only the construction's own fabric now remains, and I would not like to hazard how long that will outlast the trove that it once sheltered. The shell of it, the body alone endures; comatose, vegetative, abandoned by the inhabiting quick, its self-possession quite annihilated.

But with that loss, we gain. We are released, able finally to quit, to walk away with our hearts as well as our feet.

I step through the deserted Long Room, passing to the brittle applause of broken glass and the ferrous accolade of collapsed armour figures, fallen swords and unknown metal debris. A little moonlight is seeping from the clouds rending and departing overhead, allowing me to see. I tear one sagging hanging from a wall, gritting my teeth to the fiery handful of pain that results. I set one marble maid upon her base again and set her broken arm on the bookcase by her side; she shines milk-white in the grey-blue light, luminous and ghostly.

Stooping, I pick up a little figurine. It is a shepherdess; idealised, but still exquisitely realised and quite beautiful, as I recall. She has lost her head, and broken from her base. I squat and look about for other pieces. I find her bonnetted head, and rub a little plaster dust from her delicate features. Her nose has been chipped, its tip shining whitely through the thin blush of glaze. The head sits precariously on her slender flute of neck; I place her carefully on the bookcase shelf beside the arm of the statue then walk on, through the devastation.

. . . And find I cannot help but recall another tumultuous spoilage, long ago, instituted by Father if carried out by Mother. It was, too, the occasion of our first separation.

The memory's hazed, not so much by the accumulation of other, intervening events as due to my lack of years at the time. I remember that after the initial exchange of shouts, Mother screamed and Father only talked, that her voice assaulted the ears and that one had to strain to hear his, most of the time. I remember she threw and he ducked, or tried to catch.

We were in the nursery, playing, when we heard their voices, raised, and rising to us in that airy space of brightly painted attic. The nurse looked flustered, hearing the shouts and screams, the harsh words and accusation filtering up from the bedroom on the floor below. She went and shut the door, but still the noise came to us, carried by some by-way of the castle's much-altered geography while we played with bricks or trains or dolls. I think we looked at each other, keeping silent, and went on playing.

Until I could stand no more and ran past nurse and hauled the door open, sobbing as I ran down the narrow steps while the woman cried out after me, calling me back. She ran, following me, and you came padding behind her.

They were in his bedroom; I charged through the door just as Mother threw something at him. A piece of porcelain, part of his collection, it flew, white as a dove, across the room and smashed on the wall above his head. I think he'd made to catch it, and might have, but for my sudden appearance. He scowled at me as I ran towards my mother, crying and wailing.

She was standing by a display cabinet against one wall; he was by the door connecting to her room. He was dressed for a trip to town. She wore filmy night things under a housecoat, her hair was wild, her face striped with some beauty treatment. In her left hand she held a piece of lavender paper with writing on it.

She was not aware of me until I thudded into her thigh and clamped myself to her, begging her and Father to stop shouting, stop arguing, stop being horrible to each other. I smelled her perfume, the treasured natural odour of her and the light, flowery scent she favoured, but I detected something else too; there was another perfume, darker and muskier than hers, which I realised only later must have emanated from the sheet of mauve notepaper she held crumpled in her hand.

I thought, perhaps, that just by being there, just by reminding them of my existence I might stop them shouting, never imagining that my presence, that very existence, might itself provide a further stimulus for dispute. I did not know that the whole course of our lives from then on had been determined by two pieces of paper in that room. One – white, severe and crisply edged, folded neatly in Father's jacket – was a letter with a seal of state upon it, sending him to a foreign capital to represent his country; the other – a mauvely fragrant tissue, hotly crumpled in Mother's hand – had been hidden by Father, discovered by Mother, re-hidden by her and then revealed, minutes ago, in response. Both represented an opportunity for the holder, together they defined a calamity for our family.

She clasped me to her as I sobbed into the comforting quilt of housecoat, her balled fist – the one holding the note – pressing between my shoulder-blades and trembling. She shouted again, words tumbling fast, desperate and breathless from her mouth. Fierce, accusing, humiliated words; phrases and sentences of discovery and betrayal and abandonment and sordid, filthy acts and hate. I understood few of those words at the time, can directly remember none of them now, but their meaning, their import pierced my ears like burning spikes and blistered inside my head; I screamed for her to stop and threw my hands over my ears.

Somebody else's hands closed round me and started pulling me away. I clutched at Mother again, tighter than ever, while the nurse tried to prise me away from her and you stood in the doorway, holding on to the doorknob, dark eyes wide, calmly inquisitive.

Father's voice was measured, calm, reasonable. He spoke of duty and opportunity, of staleness and fresh starts, of the weight of the past and the promise of the future, and of tired land and new lands. That very coolness induced the opposite in Mother and his every word seemed to incite her wrath and draw still greater venom from her, wrenching each word of public responsibility from his mouth and twisting it, forcing it to the question of what was fit private behaviour and finding each one not just wanting but disgraceful.

Father made the point that we should all go; Mother screamed he would leave alone.

213

Mother's voice was becoming hoarse; she reached into the display cabinet, withdrew another figurine and threw it at Father, who caught that one and held it while he spoke in quietly reasonable tones to her. She moved, making me move with her while the nurse tried to pry my fingers from her hip; Mother put her flattened hand into the cabinet and swiped a shelf-full of the porcelain figures out, smashing and bouncing them on to the floor.

I wailed, kicked at the nurse.

You crossed the room and gently took the caught figure from Father's hand, then – as Mother threw another one over your head, which deflected off Father's outstretched arm and broke on the floor – you knelt and started picking up the broken pieces of porcelain from the floor, gathering them in your paint-spotted smock where the intact figure lay.

I think my wracking sobs must have weakened me, for finally the nurse pulled me away from Mother; the nurse gripped my hand tightly in hers and dragged me screaming, my feet pulling a rug with me, towards you. You looked up at her, then stood and carefully emptied the pieces you had gathered on to the tall bed. You took the nurse's other hand as she led you and pulled me to the door, her apologies unheard over Mother's gasping screams. The next thrown piece hit Father hard on the head. He put one hand to his brow and looked annoyed at seeing the blood smearing his fingers.

I broke away at the door and ran back; the nurse gave chase and I leapt upon and ran across the bed, scattering the porcelain pieces you'd retrieved. I ran to Father, now wanting to protect him from Mother's anger.

He pushed me away. I stood, dizzy and confused, between the two of them, staring up at him as he pointed to me and shouted something back. I remember not understanding, thinking, How could he not want me? What was wrong with me? Why would he take only you?

Mother shrieked denial; the nurse grabbed me with both hands and stuck me under her arm, supporting me on her hip; I struggled only weakly at first, still bewildered. Near the door I shook and wriggled free once more and ran back towards Father. This time he swore, took me by the scruff of the neck and marched me to the door past the crying, apologising nurse. He threw me far out into the hall. I landed at your feet. The nurse exited the room at a run and the door slammed behind her; the lock clicked.

You reached down to wipe some of Father's blood from the side of my neck.

He took you with him that day, and for the first and last time he struck his wife as she tried to keep you with her as well. She was left lying sobbing on the courtyard's stones as he led you, uncomplaining, down to the passageway, through it and over the bridge to his waiting car. I knelt by Mother, sharing her tears, and watched you and him both go.

You looked back just once, caught my gaze and smiled and waved. I think you never looked so unconcerned. My tears seemed to dry instantly, and I found myself waving feebly in return, to your back, as you skipped off.

I step to the central stair, where plaster like a fall of purer snow covers one huddled, sleeping form, which moves, mumbles in its sleep and barely disturbs the dust. Something cracks loudly under my foot as I pass by, and a drunken, incoherent challenge issues from the crumpled shape. I stand still, and the soldier sleeps again, mumbling down to silence.

I think there of laying down the pistol dangling heavy from

215

my right arm, but my damaged, burned hand has grown used to the weapon by now; clenched around its coolness, the singed flesh is uncomplaining save for a dull and distant ache; to will its motion now, to prise the weeping skin from the gun's handle and flex that cracked surface would be to invite further pain. Better, less painful, to leave it there. And anyway, who knows that the weapon might not be needed?

I walk on up the curving steps to the stairhead of the bedroom floor, where banister rails, skewed and cracked, bank out over the drop like fingers clawing at the vacant space. My feet, favouring the inner limit of the steps, scuff plaster dust with each step. The corridor brims with shadows, a dark forest of pale columns and pillars, broad patches of inky shade and slanted beams of moonlight; a winter's path through lessened debris, flanked with dark pools the colour of the backs of ancient mirrors. I hear distant grunts, a bed or floorboard creaking, someone coughing. The air smells of smoke and sweat and drink. On the floor, a flurry of unleaved books are swept and bustled along by the draught from a broken window. I follow them.

The door to my room lies ajar; more manly snores trouble the air within. In the doorway to your room, my dear – and in a projected window-shape of fallen moonlight – lies one more sleeping form, curled up in a dark sleeping bag, a steel helmet lying by his head and a gun standing balanced against the corner of the door's jamb. I walk over to him, treading carefully to avoid rustling papers and broken records and stepping over a floorboard which I know creaks. I lean closer and catch a glimpse of what, by the moonlight, may be ginger hair. Karma, then, our machine-gunner and faithful guardian of the lieutenant's sleep. I suppose I could unlock the door, but his gun would fall if I opened it. I suppose I could lift his gun away, but its strap is looped round his wrist, near where his childishly bunched fist lies by his cheek.

I retreat, to the open door of my own apartment. The darkness is filled with the snuffling, rasping noise of a drunk man in troubled sleep. There is little light; the fire is unlit, the curtains are drawn and anyway the room faces away from the moon. I slide my feet carefully. I know where everything would be in this room in normal times, but what litter has been left, what clothes dropped and furniture moved by whoever sleeps here now I cannot tell, or see.

I shuffle round the bottom of the bed and feel my way past the chest there, my fire-sensitised hand brushing against what feels like female underwear and a glass lying on its side. I cross to the wall by the connecting door. My shoes encounter broken glass, a brittle layer on the surface of the rug. The cabinet by the wall has been opened; my waving, scouting hand touches its wood and glass door and swings it closed with a gentle thud and a grinding scrape of glass. I freeze. The snoring behind me hesitates and alters in pitch a little, but still continues manfully. I feel my way to the recess of the connecting door.

Arthur's pass-key turns smoothly in the lock and makes it click. I remember that there are bolts on both sides of the door. I reach up and feel that the one on this side is unsecured. I hesitate, wondering what might turn on the turn of this handle, what the opening of this door might lead to.

The door's handle turns easily in my damaged hand, and with the gentlest of pressure, the door, heavy and thick, starts to open.

I step through, into a flame-uncertain space full of amber shadows. The door closes with barely a click.

At last, my dear. I find you and our lieutenant.

The room is lit by thick-stumped candles and the remains of

a fire in the grate, its logs reduced to deep red glowing caves in a landscape of grey and black, devoid of smoke and flame. Above each candle stands an incandescent tear-shaped glow, still as blown glass. They waver in the faint draught produced by my entrance, consecutively: first the candle on the near end of the mantelpiece, then that on a chest, then one at the far end of the fire, lastly the candle on the cabinet by the bed, where an automatic pistol lies, dark metal gleaming. The gentle tide of shadows laps at the lieutenant's skin and yours, like light stroking the smooth shapes of your shared flesh.

The lieutenant's body, one vertical half exposed, looks leaner than I'd expected. Her skin is like a child's in this light; pink-soft. You two lie together, limbs nakedly entangled, carelessly entwined in a drowsy chaos of pillows, sheets and clothes, your cheek on her shoulder, her leg thrown over your hip, one hand lying lightly on your breast. How vulnerable she looks with you, my dear, how unmouthed her commanding pride, how unlieutenant-like her exposed accessibility, how slumber-fit the cheek-conforming shoulder, the tousle of dark hair, the languid reach of out-thrown arm, the succulent curve of rump and the soft hand cupping, all spread floating upon the billowed silken sheets like bare-connected flotsam on a kind and magical sea.

How innocent, how beautiful you appear, raised above the fortified debauchery engorged in the storeys below, languorous and composed in a shared and silent peace, secure in your soft citadel of sleep. I walk carefully round to the bottom of the bed, mindful of where I know the floor creaks, ducking to prevent my candle-shadow falling across the lieutenant's serenely sleeping face.

How I ache to join you both, to slide silently in and join your warmth, to be accepted by her as well as you.

But I know this cannot be. The lieutenant's shown no sign her tastes run to such inclusion, or that she might acquiesce to what I'd wish. I must be content to have witnessed this, to have seen what's to be seen and hold the memory of it close within me. It is enough. I have no idea what this may lead to, what change in circumstance and loyalties could entail hereafter, but we long since agreed these things must be treated with a reasoned passion, and that risk run. Only our requited leeway lets us drift together, only the loosest ties will keep us bound at all. Our wide licence has been the guarantee of our relaxed affiliation, holding us within our wildly casual orbits where a narrower scope of mutual consent would quickly have torn us apart.

It was selfish of me to have intruded as much as I have. Sleep on, gentle ladies. Forgive me for taking this small amount of enjoyment from the aftermath of yours. I'll make my exit, leave you in peace and perhaps find a bed somewhere above.

I tread with due care back round the bed, again watching where I place my feet, again ducking under the line the candle-light takes from glowing wick to our lieutenant's lidded eyes.

A floorboard creaks beneath me, where none ever sounded before. Of course, I realise; I am near the rug covering the hole the shell left. The lieutenant stirs, sleepily. I take a long step off the offending board and it makes an abrupt cracking noise as it springs back into place. I hear a sudden noise behind on the bed, and start to turn, startled, off-balance, staggering and putting my foot out towards the edge of the rug, thinking it must be centred over the hole.

But something in the castle lets me down. As I look back, and see your head begin to rise and the lieutenant turning quickly round, twisting the bedclothes around with her like some spun cocoon – her eyes starting to open, her hand going

219

out towards the cabinet at the side of the bed – my foot meets the hole beneath the rug, imperfectly plugged. My leg disappears beneath, plunging me down; my other foot slides on the wooden floor as I begin to drop. My arms fly out, my hands trying to clutch at—

The gun, forgotten in my burn-frozen grip, erupts with sound. Loosed like a taloned bird to grasp the sanctuary of the mantelpiece's marble perch, my hand, fingers spasming, jerks closed instead on the pistol's trigger. The shot cracks, stupefyingly loud in the room, and a harsh spear of flame flashes from the muzzle, obliterating the soft glow of candles and log embers, blinding me. My leg catches in the hole; I twist as I fall, head hitting the metal rail at the hearth's edge; the gun is still firing, possessed of its own leaping life, its lunatic bark filling my hand and my ears. Marble cracks, splinters scatter, screams and ricochets echo somewhere within the maelstrom of noise. I roll on my back, dazed, while the gun continues to jolt and leap in my hand. Even as I fall to the floor, leg pinned, caught like an animal in a trap, I find myself wondering how the gun can still be firing, and only dimly start to understand that, unlike any gun I have ever used, it fires as long as the trigger is depressed. I tell my hand to open, will my fingers to release the trigger, as I struggle back up, trying to sit.

Then I see the lieutenant, nude and kneeling wide-legged on the bed, a pistol held in both her hands and pointing straight at me. I open my mouth, to explain. Behind – beyond her limber, pinkly splayed body – I see you, crouched, doubled over, shaking, clutching at one arm.

Is that blood there on the sheets? Did I—?

The lieutenant fires before I can speak, before I am able to explain, or question, or protest. Something smacks into the side of my head like a hammer-driven spike, spinning me, twisting me, flicking my sight about so that the candle flames' tiny points wheel and trail and make a halo round me, their little fluttering lives a lineage.

Then all light drains away entirely as I fall back once more, hitting the boards in fading silence.

Darkness. No more shots. Stillness.

I seem not to be able to hear anything directly, and yet somehow I become aware of things. I am conscious of crying, of shouts, of soothing sounds, of heavy slamming things and terrible roars and stamping, thudding noises. The existence, the presence of these sounds is reported to me somehow, but only as concepts, as abstract entities. I cannot tell who cries, who speaks or what is said or exactly what the noises are or mean.

I want to open my eyes but cannot. There is a storm coming, I think. The gun is torn from my hand. It does not hurt very much. I would like to say something, but I cannot. Something thuds into my side, into my ribs. It happens again. It takes a moment, in this enveloping darkness, for me to work out that I am being kicked. It begins to hurt a little. The crying and shouting and slamming, thudding noises continue. Is that the trees? Can I hear the trees, starting to move in the breeze? Another kick, which hurts more.

'—here!' a voice says, distinct.

Hands close around me, lift me roughly up. My leg is extricated from the hole in the floor. Then I am thrown down again, landing on something soft, I think.

I am on my back. No, my front.

I can hear confused noises now. Boards creak, doors slam, feet come clubbing; clothing noises, slippings, slidings; distant running steps, beat-broken, all heading this way; shouts puzzled, anxious, relieved and angry; urgent talking. I think

221

that we shall all be sorry when that storm descends. My head's pulled up, thumped down again. Can hear it gathering in the mountains. Oddly numb. More words. Dark amassing clouds for crowns. Still breathing. A certain darkness at the summit. Rudolph. Riduff. Rid of.

That is you crying, I believe. Comforting words from the lieutenant. I am still trying to speak because there must be things to be said. I think my eyes are open, though not because I believe I can see anything. I think I can see. I would certainly like to. Aware of many people. The room seems very red, as though observed through a mist of blood. You on the bed, huddled, being held; tended. Plaster on the floor, blood dark upon the bed. The lieutenant, sitting on the bed, pulling on a boot. Hissing light, some old gas-powered thing. There is a rug beneath me, soft soaking. Voice I recognise; a servant's, shouting, imploring, a room away, then hurried discussion, orders given and more shouts, the servant's voice protesting, quieting, going, disappearing. The storm is still coming though; its roar is loud against the castle's hollow walls.

I am wondering who screamed. Was it you, my dear, or her? Or me, perhaps? For some reason it seems important just now, this knowledge of who it was who screamed, but I know only that somebody did. I can remember that scream, recall its sound, play it back inside my head even over the roar of the storm, but from that memory it could have been any one of the three of us. Perhaps it was all of us at once. No.

'—ot here!' a voice says. But whose?

An aftermath-dark roar consumes me. Now is the storm come. The thing I hear last is, 'Not here, not *here*. Not—'

CHAPTER
SEVENTEEN

C astle, I was born in you. Now again you see me like a helpless child carried through your devastated halls. By the same litter that displaced our shell I am conveyed past the soldiery, their temporary conquests and our servants, all standing gawking. The debris I walked amongst and the sleeping forms I passed, alone animate, solely erect and balanced, scornful of their noisy lethargy only minutes ago, now drunkenly witness my expulsion, swept out impotent and disarmed. A candle apiece, that congregation watches me, like some annual virgin paraded in her garish tawdriness through the usual pious squalor.

The lieutenant spreads her arms as she strides past, forcing on her jacket. She quiets the crowd, telling them to go back to their beds, squeezing past me and my bearers, adjusting her collar as we tip downstairs. Blood rush to head. No, no, an accident. Help will be found. Know where there's a medic, found the other day. The lady wounded too but slightly. Both look worse than they are. To bed; get yourselves to bed. Sleep on. All will be well.

Do I see another face, calm, pale but composed at the stairhead as we go clattering down (white fingers on torn, dark wood, the other arm swaddled in bandages, cradled to your milky breast)? I think I do, but then the steps, in flights, turn the sight and take it from me.

The hall, level again. I see an armoured figure standing near the door, a black opera coat around its shoulders. I make to touch its hem as we pass by, arm going out in supplication, mouth working in the attempt to produce words. My arm flops down, brushing the floor, knuckles hitting the door step, cracking over it as we step outside and into the courtyard. The door is slammed on further enquiry. I hear boots running across the cobbles, then shouts and cries.

Not the well again, I try to say. I am unwell, and not long welled up. Have pity. (Perhaps I say it, I think, as they bundle me off the stretcher and drop me in the footwell of a jeep. No no, not the jeep, I'll have no truck with that; I shall travel in the van. They look at me strangely.) The bottom of the jeep smells of mud and oil. Something cold and stiff is thrown across me, over all my body, cutting out what light there is. The vehicle's suspension dips, words are muttered, a distant rattling noise is overwhelmed as the engine cranks roaring into life and starts the steel beneath me shaking.

Springs creak, air hisses; two heavy pairs of boots find footing on me, pinning my head and knees. The engine coughs and revs, gears grind and then we jerk and jolt away. The courtyard cobbles shake me, the passageway amplifies the engine's blare, then we're outside, beyond the walls, arching over the bridge – a few more shouts and a single, flat shot – and heading down the drive.

In my mind I try to follow our route, attempting to combine the map of memory with the blind movements of the jeep; here my head is forced against the sill, here the boots that rest upon me weigh more, or slip back, or slide forward. I thought I knew the lands about here well, but I believe I lose the way before we even leave our grounds. We turn left out of the drive, I think, but I am still confused. My head is hurting, and my ribs. My hands, too, still ache, which seems unfair, as though their wounds belong to a much earlier time, and ought by now to be long healed.

They mean to kill me. I think I heard them tell the servants they were taking me to a doctor, but there is no doctor. I am not being taken to be helped, unless it's to be helped to die. Whatever I was to them, I have now become nothing; not a man, not a fellow human being, just something to be got rid of. Just stuff.

The lieutenant believes I wanted to kill her, or you, my dear, or both of you. Even if I had the power of speech, there's nothing I could say to her that would not sound like a sorry excuse, a hopelessly contrived story. I wanted to see; I was inquisitive, no more. She had taken over our home, taken over you and yet still I did not resent, did not hate her. I only wanted to watch, to have confirmed, to witness, to share the tiniest part of your joy. The gun? The gun just presented itself, promiscuous in its very being, a casual pick-up, inviting the hand it's designed to fill and then – in my damaged state, stuck to it, stuck with it – easier to retain than to abandon.

I was leaving, you would never have known I was there; luck, simple fate decreed my downfall.

Not here. Not here. Did you really say that? Is that what I truly heard? The words echo in my head. Not here. Not here . . .

So cold, my dear. The words, the meaning so matter of fact, so pragmatic sounding. Did you too think I came like some covetous swain in a bitter rage to kill the two of you? Has our shared life not taught you what and who I am? Have all our judicious indiscretions, our widespread pleasurings and reciprocated liberties not convinced you of my lack of jealousy by now?

Oh, that I should have injured you, that even now you nurse that wound, however minor, at your breast, thinking that I meant it, and worse. That is what hurts, what injures me. I wish I could take and suffer the wound I so carelessly inflicted. My hands clench, beneath the stiff tarpaulin. It would seem that my hands have become my eyes, and my heart; for they both weep, and ache.

The steel floor beneath me hums and judders, the tarpaulin ripples and beats, one flapping corner continually tapping me on the shoulder like some manic boor trying to attract my attention. The noise of air rushes all around, eddying and reverberating, tearing and roaring, ferocious in its meaningless intensity and creating a calm more determined than mere stillness could have pretended to. My head buzzes, infected with all this resounding emptiness.

My right hand lies near my forehead; I find the control to move it closer, and the tarpaulin shields the movement. I touch my temple, feeling wetness, the pain of raw, scored flesh; a long, still slowly bleeding wound in a crease, a ridge along the side of my head, extending from near my eye to past my

228

ear. The blood drops from my brow. I catch a few drops and rub it between my fingers, thinking of my father.

What a sorry race we are, what sad ends we continue to contrive for all our selves. No harm meant, my dear, yet so much damage done. To you, to us, and to me, already harmed but about to be put beyond further harming. Should I go so uncomplaining to my end? I'm not sure I really have much choice.

We are all our own partisans, we are every one, when pressed, combatant, our clothes our armour, softly encasing our unsteady frames, our flesh the mortal fabric most suited to the fray. To the last man, at least, we are soldiers, and yet there are those who even in the face of death never discover the animating savagery such martial revelation demands, their particular character requiring a combination of circumstance and motive the situation has not produced. The merely cunning tyrant preys upon the tolerant intelligence of those better than they. Armies by brutality forge the brotherhood amongst their troops they should extend to all, then turn one against the other. Does our lieutenant do something similar to me? Does she have me in her spell, too? Would I have acted otherwise had she been a man? And am I to discover at my death a capacity for willing suffering, and a fatalism, I never guessed at in my life?

Perhaps the descent from property and polity to this rude cess of rule by gun has so abraded my sense of worth that I can envisage my surrender to its liquidating processes with relative equanimity; a hanging leaf that feels the storm's breath and happily lets go. I think now I may have been shortsighted not to have realised that though we live in periods of peace, they are as much the store of just their opposite as accumulated wealth, two-faced, implies impoverishment in its gift. We are the only animal naturally perverse; it ought not to come as a surprise to me that this applies as much in greater matters as it does in more intimate situations. We draw up rules for relations between systems, states and faiths, and for those between our selves, but they are written on the passing wave, and however much we dodge and gloss and wheel and skim and are adroitly gauche with our modifications, justifications and epicyclic excuses, by our own trammels we're caught at last, and tangled in our lines fall back to others, no better prepared.

Some part of me, resentful and frustrated at such forbearance, would lie here in sly deceit, gathering my strength, collecting my resources and then leaping up, startling and surprising them all, seizing a gun and turning the tables, bending them to my will, forcing them to accept my authority and take the direction I desire.

But this is not me. I am still lost within my body, communications with the useful parts still patchy, my legs twitching, hands clenched involuntary, head and ribs hurting, mouth working but only to dribble; if I tried to leap I might do no more than jerk, or even if I did leap up a child could knock me down, and should I try to grab a gun probably I'd miss, or be defeated by the button on a holster.

And even if I were well and whole and in the best of spirits I doubt I could assume the lieutenant's mantle so. These soldiers know what they want to do, they have a mission and a course, they are within their natural environment, however much they may resent it, however they may yearn for resumed civilian roles. But that civility is the only place I know where I can be be myself, the sole state that I can understand and that makes sense not just to me, but of me.

I would like to return to you, my dear, and to our castle,

and then be free to stay or go according to our desire, that is all. But would leaping up, taking a gun – in the unlikely event that I could – taking charge (just so), accomplish this? Could I kill them all, return and rescue you? Kill the lieutenant, your new lover, kill the others? I believe Mr Cuts is in the jeep too, and Karma, though I'm no more sure that they are than – if they are – how I know.

Too much impoderable. Too much to think on.

I might leap up and escape, perhaps, somehow avoid their shots and then be allowed to go, not worth the effort of pursuit. But to head where? Can I abandon you, abandon the castle? You two are my context and my society, in both of you I find and define myself. Though both may be taken, one despoiled for ever, one beguiled for the moment, still I have no real existence without you.

There is no recourse for me. The choices that have led to this conclusion lie too far back down the track, or up the stream – our view of it itself a choice – to make any difference now. If I had always been a man of action, or if I had not loved you so, or been less inquisitive, or if I had loved the castle less and quit when the quitting was easier – or loved it a little more, so that I was prepared to die there rather than hope to flee and eventually return – then I might not lie here now. Perhaps if I had been less fixed on you and on the castle, and you on me, and we had been more conventionally social creatures, less prideful in our refusal to hide what our feelings for each other were, things would have been different too.

For prideful, scornful we have been, have we not, my dear? Had we been more prudent, less disdainful, had we hidden our contempt for the trite morality of the herd and concealed our activities, we might have kept the wider pool of friends, acquaintances and contacts that gradually dried up around us

231

as the knowledge of our intimacy spread. It was not even just that awareness that gradually isolated us, it was rather the undeniability of that perception, for people will tolerate much in others, especially those others whose esteem is judged worth the winning, but only if the possessors of that knowledge can credibly pretend to themselves and others that they do not know what they really do.

That cosy self-delusion was not enough for us, however; it seemed part and parcel of the same outmoded morality we had already twice denied, through our own close but prohibited union and the wider compass of hardly less scandalous liaisons we partook in and encouraged. And so, in our vanity, having found stimulation in these earlier scandals and desirous of new ways to shock, perhaps, we made it too difficult for those around us with any regard for popular judgement to deny what we were and what we did.

We still had friends, and were received civilly enough in most of the places we had come to know, and nobody with a home like ours, with well-stocked cellars and a generous disposition ever lacks for numbers to make up a party, but nevertheless we became aware of the withering away of invitations to the other great houses as well as to the type and scale of public events where some minimal investment in the stock of moral convention is one of the conditions of entry.

At the time, we accepted our semi-outcast status with the displaced indignation of hauteur, and found no lack of eager acolytes avid to encourage such conviction. Later, as all slid down to war and the lands around us emptied, that winnowing seemed no more than an acknowledgement of our principled and brave detachment, and we professed ourselves pleased, to those still around to listen, that those fled fainthearts had finally left us alone. Later still, with only ourselves left to talk to, we stopped talking about such things, and perhaps hoped that, still and fast within our hollow home, the approaching hostilities too might ignore us, just as departing society had.

We might have done things differently. I might have done things differently. So many other choices might have led to me not lying here.

But now that I am, I know not what to do. If there is a remedy, it does not lie in my hands. And of course there is a sort of remedy, and it lies in the lieutenant's hands, and it is called her gun.

My time is come, I think, my dear. Certainly in another sense it has been and gone. I think I tried the best I could to protect you and the castle, and now, perhaps, in going to my death without complaint, I might at least take with me the comfort that I leave you, if not our home, in safer hands than mine proved to be. There may be no saving the castle; its worth is arguably half gone already just by the inner ruining of it, and it will remain conspicuous and attractive to guns as long as these troubled times persist. But for you there is hope; at the lieutenant's side, if that is the way it is to be, through the mobility, skills and ordnance of her band there may be some safety, and a sanctuary of sorts. Her arms may protect you better than mine ever did.

So little goes as we expect, and yet still I am surprised when there's a shout – the lieutenant's – and I am thrown forward suddenly, squeezed half-way beneath the seats in front while more yells ring out. Gunfire chatters in the distance, and a sequence of thuds shakes the jeep. I imagine at first that we have left the road and are suddenly pitching over a field of rocks, but something about the impacts says this is not so. We swerve violently. Shots crack out from immediately overhead, there's another sequence of piercing thuds, mixed with the sound of glass breaking and a gasp and scream, and we swerve even more violently in the opposite direction. Shouts nearby that are close to screams, then a terrific, near back-breaking crash that sets the world spinning and ignites lights at the back of my eyes. I tumble through darkness, glimpse the light of day but briefly, then something hits the back of my head and I am dimly aware of landing on something cold and damp and soft and smelling of earth with a weight pressing on my legs.

The sound of machine-gun fire blasts in around me. The acrid smell of the black powder fills my nose, making my eyes water.

'Karma?' I hear someone say, distant somehow, as though outside. I think I have my eyes open but it all seems very dark. Coldness is seeping through to my knees.

'No,' another voice says. More gunfire. Something tickling my nose may be grass. I smell fuel.

'There,' a last voice gasps; the lieutenant. 'The mill. Quick; now!'

A terrific burst of firing nearby, bringing the smell of black powder again. Then it lessens, and shortly decreases still further while the more distant fire continues. I think I can hear people running and the sound of feet thumping on the ground. I try to shift my legs; they cannot move up or down, trapped by something heavy on top of them. The smell of fuel grows greater. Gunfire still sounds all about. I begin to panic, feeling my heart beat wildly and my breathing become quick and shallow. One of my arms is trapped, too, caught between my side and something solid.

I wriggle my other hand out from hard folds of tarpaulin and find grass-covered earth near my face; I am lying on the ground, the jeep on top of me. I dig my fingers into the cold soil like talons, grip and pull with all my might. My legs slide a little; I try to kick them and attempt to find purchase with my feet. I use my trapped arm to lever myself away from whatever it's pinned against, and realise that it is my own weight that's keeping me there. Something drips on to the back of my head. The smell of fuel is growing stronger all the time. The earth thuds up at me and a sudden, sharp crack sounds like a grenade going off in the midst of the firing.

Pushing up, then clawing at the ground once more, I succeed in pulling my legs part-way through the constriction behind. My feet encounter what must be the upturned transmission tunnel; I kick and pull and heave, trying to prise my shoes off, but they refuse to move. The liquid dropping on to my head feels warm, like engine oil. I try rolling over, turning round so that my back is to the ground. My legs stay as they were, uncomfortably twisted. There is some light now. I push the tarpaulin away from my chin and reach up, finding the back of the seat in front. I haul on the seat-back and pull up on one leg with all my might. My leg comes slithering free; the other one follows a moment later. The liquid dripping from above falls on my face now, and I taste it. It is not oil or diesel fuel, but blood. I spit it out and wriggle towards the dim light, pushing the crumpling folds of the tarpaulin down around me like some discarded piece of clothing.

The edge of the jeep's bodywork stops me. There is only a hand's width of opening to the outside, where the young dawn's paleness hints at the shape of things. My panic returns with the increasing smell of diesel. I was ready to die just a couple of minutes ago, full of a fatalistic acceptance, but that was when there was no hope, and now there might be. Besides, I imagined that the lieutenant would grant me a quick death; a couple of bullets to the head and all would be over.

To die, trapped, being burned alive does not seem quite so attractive.

I make one attempt to shift the vehicle above me bodily by pushing up on all-fours before telling myself not to be stupid. Feeling around, I decide there is no other way out. Above me, by the top of the driver's seat, my hand encounters what feels like the back of somebody's head. Wedged between the seat-top and the ground, it is still warm, and the hair is matted and glued with blood. Something shifts under the hair, bone grating. I pull my hand away quickly, and a piece of fabric, cold and wet and sticky, comes with it and wraps itself round my fingers. I shake my hand, desperately trying to get rid of it. It flops by my head and in the trickle of light seeping in from outside I can just make out that it is Karma's bandana.

It seems I must make my own way out. I turn and start digging at the dew-damp ground, tearing divots of soil away from beneath the small opening. The gunfire continues unabated and another two grenade blasts erupt, the second one pattering shrapnel off the body of the jeep above me. I grip and rend and dig and push, hauling out whole clumps of grass, roots tough and straggling and snapping as they quit the cold earth, then forcing the clods of earth back past me and down and reaching back to excavate some more.

My head swims at one point, and I have to pause. The noise of firing sounds quieter, further away. I bury my face in the dirt-spattered grass beneath my face. It smells of an earthy dampness, blood, diesel and black powder. I lose myself in it for a moment. The sound of firing is less now, I'm sure. I can hear individual shots. Another grenade blast, some distance away. Using one hand, I test the trench I have gouged in the soil beneath the bodywork. A little more. I rip grass and soil away from the far side of the hole, then twist round on to my back and push up, using the transmission tunnel as a step and heaving with all my might through the grainy slickness of the soiled grass.

My head emerges into fresh, cold air; the sky above is dark grey streaked with lighter shades. My shoulders stick, wedged by the side of the jeep's body. My arms are trapped again; I shake and shimmy, feet kicking for purchase within the interior of the upside-down jeep. My head is being pushed up by the back of the hole I've dug, digging my chin into my chest. I force my head back, moaning at the pain, then kick and wriggle. My shoulders come free, I slither further out, extract my hands and push, sliding along the wet grass towards a clump of bare-leaved bushes.

CHAPTER EIGHTEEN

I lie against gnarled roots, breathing hard. I want to stand or at least sit up but the gunfire is still crackling around me and I dare not raise my head. My hands are aching; I had forgotten they were burned when I was digging with them. The jeep lies on its back on the bank of a deep roadside ditch, its rear resting in the water in the ditch's bottom, front wheels pointing at the slowly lightening clouds. The road is dotted with the litter of refugees, the jeep just one of several vehicles lying on or beside the road. Opposite me there are trees; a dark mass of conifers. Twisting and looking through the branches of the bushes, I can see a stretch of broken, sandy landscape, ridged and hummocked and scattered with low, leafless trees.

On the highest swelling of ground there is an old windmill, a black-painted clapboard construction, feathered sails tattered and forming a crucifix raised against the grey extent of sky.

Something moves against the dawn light to the east; a man running, crouched, from one low stone wall towards another. Light flickers from the open doorway of the mill. The sound of the gunfire comes at the same moment the man drops to the ground. He tries to rise, then – as the gunfire cracks again – he shakes and jerks and lies still.

Looking back, I see a dark figure moving round the side of the windmill from the other side, a rifle held one-handed, the other arm held up, hand clenched and full, by his shoulder. I squint, trying to make the fellow out in the still deficient light. I don't think he is one of the lieutenant's men. There is silence for a few moments as the man moves towards to the door. No sign of movement comes from inside the mill. The soldier edges closer, just a stride's length away.

A single shot cracks out, and the man jerks away from the side of the mill, dropping the rifle and staggering forwards as he clutches at his side. Where his side had been, against the mill's sloped wooden planks, there is a small pale gash in the black slat. He half runs, half falls past the mill's open door, arm moving, throwing something. More firing; he hops, arms flying out and for an instant he has the comical look of somebody trying to imitate the mill's shape, his spread limbs like the building's four spread sails. Then he drops, collapsing like a bag of broken bones, folding and collapsing to a sitting position on the ground outside, before toppling over and disappearing into the grass.

The explosion in the mill is a single sudden flash of light and a ragged jolt of sound. Grey-white smoke drifts out of the mill after a moment or two. I lie there for some time, waiting, but there is no more movement, no more sound.

In a little while, birdsong begins. I listen to it.

Still nobody moving. When I shiver, I decide to get up. I stand shakily, using the bushes for support, then I wipe my face with the back of a shaking hand. I remember I have a handkerchief somewhere, and finally find it. I walk across the sandy soil towards the mill, crouching and feeling foolish, but still afraid that there is somebody else here, more patient than I, lying watching and waiting with a gun. I stop by a stunted tree, gazing into the darkness of the mill's doorway. Something creaks above me. I duck and almost fall, but it is only the branches, moving in a faint breeze.

Mr Cuts lies sprawled on a barbed-wire fence just below the mill, half kneeling, arms on the far side of the wire, face laid against the barbs, the ground below him saturated with dark blood. His gun dangles from one hand, swaying in the breeze.

A little way up the slope is the soldier who threw the grenade into the mill, lying in long grass. His uniform is unfamiliar though I wouldn't be able to recognise him anyway because his face is a red ruin of bloody flesh.

I walk up to the mill and step inside. The interior reeks of smoke and a musty odour that must be ancient flour. My eyes gradually adjust to the deeper gloom. There is still dust or flour in the air, circling and settling as it backs away from the breeze from the doorway. Out of the ceiling, a single great wooden shaft descends, linked by an axle to a pair of huge and ancient millstones balanced coupled on their stony track like dancers frozen in the figure. Funnels and channels lead from hoppers to the stones, the outworks of a doubled heart. An octagonal wooden dais surrounds the great stump of rock. Not much else

243

remains, no sacks or sign of grain or recent flour; I think the mill last worked long ago.

I stumble over a couple of tape-twinned gun magazines. There is a man lying on his back by the side of the door, chest opened and bloody. Beneath the bloody, floury mask is a face I recognise as one of the lieutenant's men but cannot put a name to. By his side lies a radio, hissing. The grenade seems to have gone off a little way past him, beneath where a spiral of wooden stairs lead up into a greater darkness, their wooden steps ruptured and splintered.

By the rear of the mill's torus of stone, the lieutenant sits, her back to the wooden wall. Her legs are spread out in front of her and her head rests on her chest. Her head jerks up as I approach, and her hand comes up too, holding a pistol. I flinch, but the gun flies from her hand and clatters on to the floorboards to one side. She mutters something, then her head flops back. There is blood beneath her, its surface coated with a thin patina of flour. A grey-white dusting on her hair, skin and uniform makes her look like a ghost.

I squat by her, putting my hand to her chin and raising it. The eyes move behind their lids and her mouth works, but that is all. Blood from her nose has left twin rivulets over her lips and down her chin. I let her head fall back. The lieutenant's long gun lies nearby her hand. The exposed magazine is empty. I try various little levers and catches and eventually find the one which frees the other clip; it too has been used up. I cross to where the lieutenant's pistol lies. It feels light, though when I open it I can see there are at least two bullets in the magazine.

I look at the dead man at the door, at the two dead men visible outside, Mr Cuts hanging on the wire like an image from an earlier war, the grenade-thrower keeled over in the swaying grass with no discernible face. I hold the lieutenant's pistol in my burned, shaking hand.

What to do? What to do? Become furious, my muse murmurs, and I squat by the lieutenant again and put the muzzle of the pistol experimentally against her temple. I recall the first day we met her, when she blew out the brains of the young man with the stomach wound, after kissing him first. I think of her a little while ago, kneeling naked on the bed, firing at me, nearly killing me. My hand is shaking so much I have to steady it with my other hand. The muzzle of the gun vibrates against the skin at the side of her head, beneath her brown curls. A small vein pulses weakly under the olive surface. I swallow. My finger feels weak upon the trigger, incapable of exerting any pressure. For all I know she's dying anyway; she seems concussed or in some way losing consciousness and all this blood must indicate a serious wound somewhere. Killing her might be a release. I steady my grip and sight along the barrel, as though this makes a difference.

Then there is a creaking, cracking noise from above me, and then a disorienting sense of movement, and a deep, surrounding rumbling noise. I stare wildly around, wondering what's happening, and see the world outside the door moving, and cannot believe my eyes, and only then realise that the mill itself is rotating. The force of the breeze must have just become sufficient to make the airy wooden circle turn to face into the flow of air. Grinding and resounding, with many a mournful-sounding moan and painful creak, the mill turns, and – as though its sails and gears and stones are lode – eventually it settles its face towards the bitter north. I watch the view through the door change, sliding away from the road and the forest on its far side, taking away the sight of the dead men and gradually slowing and steadying and grumbling to a stop, to display the way west, back down the road it seems I'm fated never to travel to the end of but always to return down, the road back to the castle.

I look again at the lieutenant. The breeze tumbles in through the open door and disturbs her flour-greyed curls. I put down the gun. I cannot do this. Walking to the doorway, feeling faint and dizzy again, I look out into the dawning day and take some deep breaths. The ragged, half-empty arms of the sails are lifted as though in vain entreaty to the wind, feathered and powerless.

And yet, some part of me still says: Exert, assert your self . . . but does so too well, its sentence pronounced too clearly. I do not know, I cannot impersonate such vivacious anger. It is known to me empirically, but no more, and that knowledge pins me.

I look back at her. What would she do? And yet, should I even care what she would do? She sits there, nearer death than she can know, and in my power. I am in control, I have prevailed, even if only by luck. What would I do? What should I do? Be like myself, act as normal? And yet what is ever normal, and what value or utility has normality in these abnormal times? Less than nothing, it seems to me. Therefore act abnormally, act differently, be irregular.

The lieutenant deserves my ire for all she's taken from us, including the chance that we had to escape, those few days ago when she stopped us on this same road. That first interference led to all the rest; to the taking of our home, the destruction of our family's inheritance, to the lieutenant taking my place with you and – as must have been her intent – my planned murder. That first shot of hers, that spun me, dropped me; that was in the heat of the moment. But when they put me in the jeep, took me away from the castle, in the traditional hour of execution, that was cold-blooded, my dear.

The tolerance I've exhibited and felt towards our lieutenant has been a relic of more civilised times, when the ease of peace means we may allow each other such genteel leeway. I thought, through a display of civility, to show my contempt for these desperate days and our lieutenant's brash assumptions, but forced beyond a certain point, such politeness becomes self-defeating. I must allow myself to be infected by the violent nature of the times, to suck in their contaminating breath, take on their fatal contagion. I look at the gun in my hand. Still, this is the lieutenant's way. To kill her with the weapon she might have used to kill me might be poetic – just or not – but it seems like too easy a rhyme to me.

The wind caresses my cheek and tugs at my hair. The mill flexes, seems about to move again, then settles once more. I put the gun down on the floor, then pick it up again, check that its safety-catch is on and stuff it in the waistband of my trousers at the small of my back. I look quickly about, searching for a lever, some control.

I run up the splintered stairs, going briefly dizzy with the sudden effort, then in the upper darkness of wooden gears and spars and bins and hoppers, at last I find a wooden lever like something out of an old railway signal-box, attached by rusted iron rods to a wooden iris in the mill's wall pierced by a horizontal axle that disappears through it to the outside. I pull the wooden handle. A noise like a sigh, and a groan. A sensation of tapped power shakes the mill, and the horizontal shaft starts to rotate slowly, turning the creaking, grinding, wood-toothed gears that convert the power from horizontal to vertical and send it to the floor below, and to the stones. I race back down again, almost falling at the bottom in my haste.

The great millstones are trundling slowly round their track, shaking the whole mill with their low, deliberate thunder. They slow perceptibly as I watch, the wind outside losing some strength, then slowly they speed up again as it stiffens once more. Here is a different end, here is a fitter poesy. A strange excitement shakes me and sweat breaks on my brow. I must do this while the resolution still burns in me.

My hands slip easily under the lieutenant's armpits and I pull her up. She makes a small moaning sound. I place her by the great stone circle of the mill-wheels' track, kneeling her before it like some votary in a temple. I take the weight of her upper body, preventing her from collapsing. One flank of her is wet with blood. A wheel passes slowly in front of her on the track. My hands shake as I hold her there, letting the great stone pass, then I let her fold forward, her shoulders on the edge of the track, her head lying on it like a sacrifice. I lean back, my heart hammering violently; the next stone wheel rumbles round, ponderous and lethargic towards the lieutenant's skull, casting a shadow over her head. I close my eyes.

A terrible, grinding noise shakes me, and then the noise stops. I open my eyes. The lieutenant lies, her head caught, wedged between millstone and track, but intact. I think I hear her make a whimpering noise. I spin round to the door. A weak breeze pants at holed sails, impotent and denied. I leap up and try to shift the stones, move them back so that her head will be freed, but they refuse to shift. I quiver with rage, shout out and try to push them the other way, to crush her skull with my own strength, but even so I know I do not push with all my might, and the result is the same, and she stays, stuck but uncrushed, her head stopping the stones.

What am I trying to do? Could I remove her now in any event, bring her round and say sorry? Or will I live with the memory of the stones moving, her brains splattering? I laugh, I admit; there is nothing more to be done. I cannot kill her and I cannot free her. The radio lying near the body by the door makes a sudden crackling noise. I back away from the lieutenant, leaving her kneeling there, pressed and held, a supplicant half prostrate before the round altar of stone. At the door of that extemporised fort I turn to the breeze, then leap out, running away, turning my face to the wind and to you, my castle.

Cold rain meets me, my dear, but I set my face to you alike with that battered wooden tower, and drops in the breeze's hidden surfaces give me tears at last for all of us. I stop at the jeep, as though this last mode of transport could somehow bless my journey, but it has nothing to offer me. I take to the road alone in that cold dawn and by those wasted fields in that rain-seeded air I walk.

We are liquid beings, my dear, born between two waters, and that infectious rain seemed then like something sent from you and its eye-made strands there for me to hold and be guided by. My spirits, away from that fabrication of wood and stone, begin to lift, at the thought of returning to you. I thought I never would, but now again I have the chance. I can find a way in, or wait for the lieutenant's men to leave, leaderless and fleeing. I can reclaim you if you'll let me.

I think, just for a moment, that I hear a scream, following me from the mill, and I turn to look back at it again, but it has to fight the sounds of the rain and may only have been the radio again, and besides I was not sure I heard it at all; I turn towards the castle once more, head down against the shower.

I do believe I have an aim at last; to take you away, with no chattels and no intention of ever returning to the place that's been our home. The lieutenant and her men relieved us of all our fragile goods and our loyalty to the castle's stones, and so cast us together and alone into the free air of flight, at last alive to its pervasive force in all its wayward eloquence. The lieutenant's light fingers might have stolen you from me a little while, but you'll be mine again as you have been before.

Walk me, walk me, wind. Lead by your resistance and take me to my darling one, conduct me to our keep, my perfectly faithless refugee. The ring, I think, stopping.

I should have taken the ring of white gold and ruby that was on the lieutenant's hand, the one she took from you that first day, in the carriage on our way back along this very road. I look back, hesitating.

I hear an engine noise just then, from the direction I've been heading in. I take shelter behind an old-fashioned horse-drawn cart lying pushed on to its side by the road, one big, wood-spoked wheel raised to the sky. The engine sound comes from one of the lieutenant's trucks, an olive face with a rictus grinning grille and two bright headlight eyes. It charges past my hiding place, trailing clouds of wind-caught spray behind, its wheels making a tearing noise at the road surface. The canvas-cover over the steel frame flaps and cracks in the slipstream as it roars past. I glimpse men sitting inside, huddled busy over weapons.

I stand out beside the cart, watching over it as the truck races down the road in the direction of the mill. The truck's own wind and shower envelop me, rocking me, until the freshened breeze comes back. I decide I will not be ashamed of the relief I feel now at the prospect of hers. Let them find her; let them rescue her. She deserves no less, I suppose. It was a foolishness to treat her so. The trees behind me creak, some old leaves are scattered up from out of a ditch and another cold gust sways me, makes me shiver.

The truck's brakelights blaze, and it stops, near the distant, canted jeep. Trees between me and the mill bow, slowly, then flex back, and from their dark heads beat black bird shapes.

The truck, made tiny by the distance, reverses closer to the mill. I turn and look west, to the castle, and the rain stings me, wind gusting again. The truck has stopped. Men are jumping down. Then a sound comes from right beside me, and I jump, hand shakily to my back, feeling for the pistol wedged there.

But it is just an old piece of rag, some shred of sacking caught on the wheel of the ancient cart, and catching the wind now, too, and turning the wheel.

I wipe my eyes and watch the small figures running up towards the mill, jumping from the truck, leaping the ditch, vaulting the walls, running across the intervening ground, stopping, leaping, running, running up, the first of them just approaching the doorway of the mill.

Where the wooden arms, though broken, though only half set, though ragged with their holed fabric, still sail their course round now, and free at last salute the passing air.

I turn my back, and run, along the road at first, then when that turns, still straight for you, heading over fields and through woods, through the cutting rain and choking wind, and see it all and see nothing, forever before my eyes the sight of those wasted windmill arms, saluting and saluting and saluting.

CHAPTER NINETEEN

I climb banks, cross fences, wade streams. I am brushed and caught by twigs and branches and dying leaves. Wild animals scatter, birds startle and fly up and after me my breath trails, punctured by the rain, disappearing in its quiet bombardment. I run and jump and stagger, crashing through branches, hedges and clumps of dormant grass, plunging amongst all the brittle store of winter's promise until I see the castle.

The castle; talisman, emblem, it rises grey on grey from the dripping trees before me, for this moment in the coldly hazing rain looking not like a thing formed from the earth at all, but rather a figment of the cloud, something dreamed from the mist-invested air.

I cross the old footbridge by the orchard, its suspended timbers squealing and left jerking on their wires. I pass the walled garden, orangerie, potting sheds, the naked ornamental trees, smashed greenhouses, stoved-in cold frames, piles of decaying timbers and small darkened out-houses, the ground before them littered with cans, old wheels, sticks and splinters, pots and pans. I run with tired, failing legs and a pounding head and a breath-raw throat; I run over the moss-upholstered stones, fallen slates, sodden piles of old sawdust, and come out, finally, by the side of the castle.

All looks peaceful. One truck stands before the moat bridge. On the lawns, the refugees' camp gives up a little pale-blue smoke that mingles with the rain. I can see nobody. Even the looters seem to have deserted their posts, no longer hanging from the tower and leaving the limply flapping weight of the old snow-tiger's skin alone to greet the day.

I fall back into the bushes, my chest heaving, my breath gathering in the air above me while I try to recover some strength and work out what to do next.

The rain, ubiquitous in its interest, drifting unimpeded from the brought-down weight of sky, soaks me again and again, dripping from the dark and naked branches, shaken from the few last leaves turned the colours of decay, their ragged shapes like twisted hands, still hanging on, but troubled, disturbed and restless in the visiting wind. Gusts strafe the smoke rising from the tents and make the branches over me clatter and creak.

I haul myself up, and kneel, and soak in the castle's every detail; the rain-darkened stones, the scatter of small windows, the hole in the roof where a grey tarpaulin flaps, and on the further tower, that drenched and tattering skin, rain exploding from its striped surface with every gusting wave, and it seems to me that I can take in every chipped and levered stone, see them all spread out in plan and elevation before me, made a diagram of in my mind.

Move, I tell my quivering, exhausted body. Move now. But it needs more, requires longer, still cannot function fully yet. I take out the automatic pistol, as though its steely heft will infect me with its purpose. My hands hurt, my head aches, the rain washing at the wound. My legs grow stiff. I shiver, and gaze with a dazed incredulity at the vapours rising from my legs and face and hands and body, thinking that this steamy veil is like my body evaporating, my determination dissolving in the rain. Then the wind curls and rushes down again and sweeps my self-made shroud away.

I scan the castle's windows and battlements for you, my dear, desperate to see your face. Look down, look down, why don't you, and see one the lieutenant would be proud of, see one like her, a murderer now, like her filmy spirit, like a wraith returned, hidden in the bushes with a gun, covered in mud and leaves, by battle and by bullet scarred, and planning an attack and liberation; no natural refugee at all, but rather one become soldier, for you.

Noise grows ordered from the rain's grey hiss, gathering and swelling beyond the castle. I recognise that rising, falling, shifting engine sound, and then hear the truck's horn, flat and blaring, still some way down the drive. I run out from the bushes, stumbling and slipping over the rain-slickened grass, heading for the front of the castle and the bridge over the moat. They must have left quickly, summoned on the radio; it could be they all went, and perhaps they left the castle unsecured. I skid on the gravel and almost fall. I run past the truck, over the bridge and into the passageway. The portcullis' iron grid blocks the way; I shake it and try to lift it, in vain. Behind me, I can hear the truck's engine, growing louder.

Across the other side of the courtyard, just visible beyond the captured gun, a soldier comes out of the main door. I go still. He peers at me, then goes back in and reappears suddenly with a rifle, levelling it at me from the shelter of the doorway. It does not even occur to me to shoot at him with the pistol I am holding. Instead I duck, turn and run; the rifle shot kicks stone chips off the passageway wall as I sprint out across the bridge. The truck is coming up the drive, lights blazing. Somebody leans out of one window, sighting on me. I hear another shot.

I try the door of the parked truck, but it is locked. I run across the gravel path to the slope of grass that drops to the moat, thinking to use the bank as cover, but the grass is too wet; I make only a few steps along the slope before I slip and slide down the grass. I fall into the moat, splashing and struggling, gasping in that icy grip, trying to find some footing in the steep underwater slope beneath, still holding the pistol and with my other hand attempting to grab the grass and soil to pull myself out.

The water kicks and splashes by me; I turn, back against the grassy bank, and look up. A soldier is leaning over the battlements above, pointing a gun down at me. He waves, calls something out. I steady myself as best I can and take aim; the pistol punches back at me; once, twice, then stops. Flakes of stone puff out from the top of the wall. I pull the trigger a few more times, then throw the useless gun away. The soldier has disappeared, but now he comes back; peeking, then leaning over the parapet and shouting something down. I turn my back, and with both hands start to haul myself out of the moat, waiting all the time for the shot, the awful crashing mallet-kick of a bullet hitting. Instead, there is only laughter.

Scrambling slowly, helplessly awkward in my water-weighted clothes, I pull and kick my way out of the water and up the bank. A bottle sails down, thuds off the grass nearby and plops into the moat behind. I reach the gravel path and stand, swaying and looking up at the battlements. The soldier there waves again. The two trucks are parked together now. A few of the soldiers are lowering something from the rear of the truck that's just returned; some are standing watching me. Another bottle sails out from the battlements, arcing down to shatter on the gravel near my feet. One of the soldiers at the trucks starts walking towards me, making a beckoning motion with his rifle. I run for the trees.

Then as I run across the lawn I hear a shout, and look back to see the soldier returning to the truck. The soldiers do not follow me, or shoot at me. They troop into the castle.

I squat in the bushes, shivering, my body aching with cold. I shake uncontrollably, trying to believe I shall ever be warm again. On the battlements, a drunken soldier waves a bottle at me, then looks behind and walks away. I look down, on all-fours, panting like a frustrated lover at the unresponsive ground, my breath blown back at me. Even this pathetic posture cannot be maintained, my arms and legs both giving way; I have to curl up on my side, quivering in the bushes like a shocked and wounded animal.

I had thought I had been quite dashing enough, but the castle fails me. I am locked out, the soldiers, whether they know it was I who killed their lieutenant or not, seem unconcerned with me, not judging me worth the effort of pursuit. And you, my dear, you are nowhere to be seen. The pistol was no use; two pointless shots, then nothing. And what good could

I have done with the thing in any event? Crutch, gravestone, pipe, club, spear; guns have many uses, multifarious effects. Perhaps they alter minds as well as anatomies; perhaps their ejected issuings get under the skin in more ways than one. Do they determine more than those who fire them? Do their unmuzzled mouths really speak so loud, their barrels overflow with death and mutilation with such effect that they speak louder than we, who, recoiling from their use, cannot see that more damage is done behind them than before?

But the lieutenant—

But the lieutenant is dead, and so no good example. Did I kill her by being different, or the same? It hardly matters, and anyway I threw the gun away.

Now I hear more shouts from the castle. I rise to my knees, still unable to stand. The cold seems to penetrate to my bowels; I do not think I can run away. Guns fire, but only into the air.

They stand behind the battlements; nearly all her men, and some of the women from the camp as well. The grey folds of rain descend between us, but I can see it all; the chipped stones, the waving, saturated skin, the holed roof, and that line of ill-matched men and women, most drunk and swaying, some of them waving, some smiling, some shouting, some firing their guns into the air.

They have you both. Until this moment there was some part of my mind that wanted to believe that the lieutenant did not really die, that she extricated herself before the wind set the millstones moving, that a soldier I hadn't noticed made it to the mill before those arms sailed round, that some unclutching in the mill's mechanism had let the sails move while the stones stayed still. That same desperate site of hope within my mind deluded itself with dreams of you having stolen away from the castle already, not sanguine about my fate – as you seemed – at all, but secretly appalled at what you knew the lieutenant intended for me and determined to make your escape from the castle and her control.

Fantasies, my dear, and me all the more pitiful for imagining that not thinking such thoughts openly would somehow give them a better chance of reflecting the actuality of our circumstances. Instead, there stands the lieutenant, her headless body supported by a couple of her men. Somebody behind her puts a cap or beret on what's left of her neck. I think some of the men are laughing.

Two of the soldiers force you – quiet, expression blank – up to teeter on the rampart stones, your hair soaked blackly to your white nightdress. The nightdress clings skinlike in the soaking rain, and you stand there, arms held behind you, staring out, at once waif and voluptuary.

They pull you back down; I see the nightdress thrown up over your head as they force you back against the parapet, your head between two of the stones. There is some shouting and jeering. I find myself biting my lip, only realising that I am doing so when the blood is sucked back into my mouth.

I do not think you afford the soldiers much sport, or perhaps their women prevail on most of them; at any rate, within a few minutes you are lifted back up to the parapet again, expression still unreadable. I think I see a trickle of blood on your chin, too. They are tying your arms behind your back; a length of bandage trails slackly from your right forearm. I believe I see you shiver.

The men are shouting and yelling, calling on me to come out. I try to rise, but then fall back, paralysed by the cold and the realisation of my own wretched helplessness.

The lieutenant's body is anointed with some wine, then

pushed over the edge of the parapet; it falls, somersaulting slackly and splashes out of sight. You stand, my dear, helpless as I, your eyes as empty as my mind is of ideas that might save us. Some refugees – men, old women and children – come round from the front of the castle, hesitant, uncertain, but drawn by the calls and laughter and harmless fire and the sound of the young women on the battlements joining in. Most gather on the gravel path, though some hang further back, still fearful. I watch the men at the battlements, I watch the castle, its skin flag flapping, I watch the rain, and a dark bird that circles, high above, and which may be one of mine, a freed raptor returned at last.

Only you I cannot watch; that awful blankness drives my sight away, forces down or up or to the side my feeble gaze. That face has been my vanity's mirror; on it you have let me write anything I have ever wanted to write, shown me anything I have ever wanted to see. Now, like the blind spot in the eye that lets us see at all, it is the one place I cannot look, the one sight I cannot bring myself to take in.

They gasp. The crowd gasps, seeing you fall, a slick white flame fluttering to the moat.

I run out again, as amazed at my lack of control over this action as I am at my sudden strength. The soldiers do not fire.

I run past a few of these dispossessed people, pushing through, stumbling to the bank of the moat. Your head only shows, set in that chopping, disturbed surface like an answer to the headless body floating near, still bobbing in the waves caused by your fall. You cough and spit, struggling. People by me mutter. I look up and see a rope leading from near your head up to the battlements. Someone pulls it tight and your head disappears, pulled underneath. Your tied feet are pulled out, jerking, then your legs, naked and kicking, all pulled on that rope until your head alone is left underwater and your body is left twisting on the rope, exposed for all to see.

You buck, doubling, raising your head out, pale body naked, head and hair covered by the long white shroud of the soaked nightdress caught round your neck; it flaps, drips and ripples, pale and sinuous as your stretched body. They drop you again. You splash and go under; the nightdress floats around you like a lily, then you rise to the air, gasping. The rope's pulled tight once more and you disappear again, head pulled under.

I hear myself shouting to them, beseeching them to stop, to let you go. I try to remember their names, but I am not sure that I do: 'Deathlock! Twotrack!' I call to them, but they cheer and laugh and bob you down and up again on their rope.

I run forward, sliding and falling down the slope of grass into the water. The men whoop and holler as I hit the moat; I reach out, trying to get hold of you as you double-up again and raise your head out of the waves, but they move you along, out of my grasp, cheering and firing their guns into the air again. I kick out towards you, swimming, oblivious of cold or fatigue, fingers clawing out towards you.

Somebody moves on the bank, one of the refugees shouting to me and starting to scramble down the grass, holding something out towards me. Warning shouts come from above, and then shots crack out above and the water in front of the man flicks up in tall splashes. He is helped back up the grassy slope by those on the path; they're moving round, following you as the soldiers dip you under again and I thrash after you.

I grab the edge of your nightdress and try to pull you to me, but they haul you further along, towards the corner of the castle and the moat, and the nightdress rips and tears, falling from you. I swim through it and it catches on me, holding me, slowing me. The soldiers jeer and laugh. You bump against the wall, then you are sent under again, then pulled out, spluttering, bending weakly at the waist once more, your revealed face flushed with strain, your voice still unheard.

I move again, and again, and the water swirls about me, a livid, pressing well of cold, draining warmth, strength, breath, thought and life all out of me. My nails dig at the hard, chill slime of the castle's stones, the still snagged nightdress and my saturated clothes pulling me back and down. We move round the corner, the crowd following, the soldiers taking turns to drag you, lower you and pull you out, throwing bottles to splash near me, laughing and shouting. I swallow air, swallow water, flap hopeless at the dark waves, falling behind, while they move you, scraping your nakedness along the rough stones to the next corner. You are barely struggling now; your splutterings sound desperate and shrill, asthmatic. Mockingly encouraging shouts sound from above as I struggle uncoordinated through the sapping cold of the water and the refugees rush to follow your dangling, silent form to the next corner, and then round it, disappearing.

My fingers, burnt, frozen, claw at the slimy stones and drag me slowly on, still impotently pulling your nightdress after me, to the corner's bulking edge. I round it.

The soldiers are silent, standing quiet and still above as the people stand below on the gravel path.

You hang in the water, suspended by the ankles, your only motion a slow twisting and untwisting on that rope, turning your body from breasts to feet away from and then back towards the castle, your head, shoulders and hair submerged in the moat's quiet circumference.

I shiver, then push, bumping between the three rotting

corpses of the looters. I float towards you. And we, in our suspended state, meet gently.

I touch your cold head and raise it out. Your eyes still stare; water dribbles from your mouth and pools in your nostrils. The rain falls softly all around us.

A heave on the rope, and you are taken from me, the head I cradled hauled up, bumping off the stones, jerking dripping away, your black hair in straight lines dropping long and soft inside the rain's rough sympathy. Those drops strike my face, and the soldiers pull you over the edge, then spit down at me.

I drift back, hitting the soft bank, turning. The refugees look down, look up, then two reach down and help me out, near the bridge; the nightdress stays in the water, floating. At the gravel summit of the bank, I stagger and cannot stand; the two who have helped me have me sit on the grass bank and an old coat is put around me; then shouts and shots scatter them, sending them back to their camp. I try to rise again, thinking that I might still somehow escape, but I succeed only in getting to my knees, and end up kneeling in the shadow of the trucks, on the gravel before the curved cobbles of the moat's bridge.

They untie the tiger skin and throw it down, flopping wetly on to the grass. They tie you there instead, pulling down so that you are hoisted up, bowing the flagpole, bumping against it as they raise you feet first to its top and tie the lanyard. You hang, still twisting and untwisting, offered to unbounded depths of sky.

The soldiers desert the roof and, soon, some smoke drifts up.

The grey wisps turn black, filling the air around you, the rolling tumbling locks and curls of black being caught and blown away by the dampening wind.

I see you, unseeing, disappearing white in grey and black. I lower my head, and by and by, small flakes of soot drift down and cover me.

The people fall back to their tents and carts, some striking camp, some already on their way. Rain and cold moatwater drip from me. The portcullis groans and scrapes, and engines start. One of the soldiers walks out to me, takes me by the elbow and supports me as I stagger, then guides me almost kindly back across the bridge. I want to break away, to run for my life, or dash out to the refugees, to shout and wail and demand their help, or somehow to shame the soldiers into a show of contrition or regret, but I have no strength left, no warmth for you or me or anybody or anything else.

The other soldiers meet me, show me my castle all dressed in flames, fire leaping exultant from every door and window, then with their trucks and jeeps and the gun, they leave the place to blaze and smoke and take me with them out of it.

I see you through the fire, I think, cold and white and in a still point poised, untouched between those warring tides, at full mast floating in that swift, turmoiling mix, flying in the wind's swift gust, and all downfalls at once saluting.

CHAPTER TWENTY

A nd now, my dear, I'm finished. The tale is done, and done with us as it would. There has been an evening, and with the dawn comes worse. I watch the day die slowly, the sunset's gaudy show dragging clouds down with it and finally outdoing the castle's last weak glow.

A bird of prey, returning hunter, is circling and wheeling, rising and falling over the last surrendered warmth our home breathes up, cutting edges through that quiet grey smoke and surfacing beyond and banking back.

A hawk, I do believe. One of mine I let fly out, come back. I gaze up, submitting for a moment to an easy admiration of the beast, imagining that it knows somehow that I am here and you are not and all is lost, that some honed slayer's instinct brings it back to acknowledge all our fates.

But it is just a bird, and stupid in our terms; its delicately fierce frame, that narrow-pared skull, holds just sufficient sense for its carnivorous function, and contains no room for any further thought. Carved to fit its place in life through the struggles of all its ancestors, sculpted by the vast simplicity of evolution it has no more sense of our tribulations than does a knife, or a bullet, and is just as blameless. What we call its cruel beauty appeals to our found sense of awe, but it is our pride, our ferocity and our grace that we deify in it, and at our peril forget it is that saving subtlety of mind that lets us think at all which we put below the talon's crude mechanic grasp, and – precisely by our reckoning – it is we who remain forever above it.

I hear the sound of other guns, that great rumble rolling over the land from some distant front, somehow surprising me, forcing the unknowing world back upon my consciousness, as I stand here; bound, condemned and waiting.

The soldiers say they will move on tomorrow. They shooed the refugees away to take over their mean camp upon the lawns, and now a couple of husbands and one of our servants float in the moat too. You, forever silent one, are still raised up within the clearing air, poised blackened over the collapsed and gutted shell of the castle, your composed eyes at last observing dryly what the air now offers you, and I wonder will the hawk, preferring cooked or undone meat, visit you or I.

For I too am tied, in Mezentian hyperbole, made a toy, a puppet of before the cannon's mouth. They tied me here by arms and legs and body, the artillery piece's broad muzzle in the small of my back – a larger, more potent gun, where there was a smaller one – fixing me like a sacrifice from an airy altar rifled, cross-bowed like an unknown quantity, a wrong answer, a kiss at the bottom of a page, like a mill's limbs, indeed, but unrevolving. I have been more comfortable, it is true, but I can lean back on the steel tube of the gun to take the weight off my splayed legs. My arms, pulled back by the ropes, have gone numb and so at least no longer hurt, and the men threw a blanket and a coat over me, so I should not die too soon. I was even fed some bread and a little wine.

All my attempts at playing the man of action, the lieutenant's murder and the responsibility for yours, secured me just one more day of life, and cost us everything. Their intention, at the next day's light, is to raise me to the skies, elevate me, spread over the gun's great snout, set a charge but no shell in the breach and then throw dice for which one gets to pull the firing lanyard.

I made my pleas, I tried to reason, to appeal somehow, but they see a fitness in my death, I think, that is not entirely predicated upon their – admittedly correct – conviction that it was I who killed the lieutenant. My pleas were too eloquent, perhaps, my attempt to use reason doomed from the start, and as for my try at appealing to them man-to-man – as a chap unjustly accused, a chum, a mate in trouble – that was, apparently, just laughable (for certainly they laughed).

Still, for all my fear – felt in the guts that will bear the brunt of my release – I think I can still savour the fact that my life ends with a blank, and see the possibilities for touches the soldiers might not appreciate. And so I want the hawk to come down and peck some living part of me, or the soldiers to raise me up now, place an old tin helmet on my head, sponge some water into my mouth and stick a bayonet in my side . . . But I am any-way between these thieves, and a calm eye in the circle of their vehicles, something they have already grown bored with.

271

The hawk settles on you, my dear. I try to watch it perch and pull and pluck and tear with a disinterested eye, but find the exercise impossible, and have to look away, at the bare trees and the dark tents and the remainder of the lieutenant's men.

They are busy finishing off the castle's last reserves, consuming its food and wine or busy with the women they decided to keep from the camp. Tomorrow they may fire a few more rounds back at some hazy westward front, and then retreat, but perhaps not.

There have been arguments. They seem uncertain, now. Some want to abandon the gun entirely, thinking it might slow them down, complaining that they have nothing they particularly want to target. Others want to offer their services to a larger concern, or find some other shelter, citadel or town which they can threaten with the gun, and so be paid for sparing.

I do not understand their war, nor know now who fights whom for what or why. This could be any place or time, and any cause could bring the same results, the same ends, loose or met, or won or lost.

I look around their appropriated camp and see them, quiet or snoring, stoking a fire, smoking the lieutenant's dry cigarettes, guzzling their booty, checking their weapons or with their women.

I am too tolerant, I suspect, for the truth is that I feel sorry for these brutes. They kill me now but they'll die later, writhing on the blood-muddied ground with no lieutenant there to kiss them and then swiftly dispatch; or they'll live limbless, institutionalised, with a ghost of pain forever haunting the abbreviated memory of flesh, or carry the wounds deeper still, in the abyssal darkness of the mind, and toss tormented by the dreams of death decades hence, alone in their sleep no matter who lies by their side, transported by the recollecting claws of that embedded horror back to a time they thought they'd lived through and escaped, forever dragged back and down.

It is my estimation that, unless one's involvement is peripheral, nobody survives a war; the people who come out the other side are not those who went in. Oh, I know, we all change, every day, and each morning emerge from our cocoon of sleep a different person, to confront an unutterably alien face, and any illness, and all shocks, age and change us by their given degrees . . . yet when the illness is past or the shock faded, we rejoin, more or less, the same society that we left, and recalibrate our selves by it. Such triangulating solace is denied us when that community itself has changed as much as or more than we have ourselves, and we must remake our own beings as well as the fabric of that shared world.

And the soldier, giving up his place in the braided stream of citizenry to be disposed into martial rank and file, surrenders more than any to the vagaries of that turmoil. The refugees, collectivised by misery and mischance, take their lives with them when they move, with some practical, if also partial hope of later resurrection; when soldiers take the lives of others, and have theirs taken, they go to their cold ends not to be commended or condemned, or contemplate a life so stamped with error, but merely to embrace the empty truth of the mind's obliteration.

Dear lieutenant, I think we all seduced you, deflected you from a course that might have let you live. Seeking something in the quick of us, searching to secure a kind of love with the provenance of age and land and family, you took over our premises; you presumed to the legacy that was ours, and if you did not see that such assumptions have their own ramifying repercussions, and that the stones demand

273

their own continuity of blood, if you did not understand the gravity of their isolation, the solitude of their trapped state or the hardness of their old responsibility, still you cannot fault the castle or either one of us, or complain that you were led to your own conclusion.

I left the castle; you brought us all back.

The night comes deeper on them and they shelter, in their tents and trucks, closer to me. My body aches from far away, displaced by time and cold. I still believe the hawk will come and be my deliverance, pecking out my eyes in some final unmeant extension of torment, or perhaps instead it will deliver me, stabbing at my bonds, fraying the ropes, freeing me from the ties that bind me so that I might have one final attempt of my own at flight.

... But the dawn is my more likely release. Or I might – ignominious, this – succumb to exposure sometime inside the night's cold kiss, relinquishing, like the castle, my last warmth to the wrapping sump of moving air.

I ought to shout and scream and curse, hurl imprecations at these fools, at least disturb the wretches' sleep on my last night, but I fear what other torture they might devise if I annoy them so, for from what I've heard and read and seen, the brutalised man, so deficient in every other type of imagination, displays a fine resourcefulness when it comes to concocting ingenious ways to hurt.

I can blame none of us, and everyone. We are all the dead and dying, we are all the walking wounded. The three of us, this ruined castle, these sad warriors, we none of us deserve our ends in this, but should not be surprised by that; it's a cause for remark, even celebration, when someone does receive their just deserts.

Castle, you should never have burned. That mill was tinder; kindling filled with air. You were stone. You felt the earthy rumble from its revolving wheels with ancient scorn, and yet you burned in its place, and now stand, but for your caved-in, black-raftered skull, looking hardly altered from this outward, down-dimmed view, but gutted, all the same, as I shall be soon. They have told me that they might set charges, to level you completely, but I think that it was said more to bring me down, rather than you. Would they waste good explosive, just to waste you? I don't believe so.

Castle, I did you a disservice saying that this could be any time; once your stones would have ensured protection as well anything might, but in the days of cannons and artillery, you only swing them to you, like compasses the loaded guns, and bring that fire down upon you all the quicker.

Perhaps we destroyed what you were a part of the instant steel struck stone in quarries, and mason's hammer and cannon's shell compound the injury alike. All is construction in the end, including this; a dying man addressing a burned-out building. My ultimate mistake, my final folly. But then we are the naming beast, the animal that thinks with language, and all about us is called what we so choose, for lack of better terms, and everything we name means – as far as we are concerned – just what we want it to connote. And there is, anyway, a reciprocity of insult for our name-calling here; for our fine, defining words tame nothing in the end, and should we ever fall victim to the unseen grammar of our life, we must brave the elements and suffer their indifference, full requited, in return.

The hawk is gone now. The descending darkness leaves you hanging alone like a single pale flame poised above the castle's husk, barely touched by a deep ruby glow emitted from the embers deep inside. Perhaps still the bird will return and peck my bindings loose, or maybe the remainder of those whose gun this was – and who may well have been the lieutenant's ambushers this morning, on the road – will suddenly attack, prevail against my tormentors and then free me, all overcome with gratitude and acknowledgement. Or the chilling wind and thickened cloud may presage snow, which will drift down and cover me and soften the contours of everything around, including the hearts of the soldiers here, so they'll take pity on me, and let me go.

Do I want an end too tidy? Or too loose? I do not know, my dears, though an answer will dawn on me, no doubt.

I think I want my death, now. Do I? Am I paradoxical? We are all that, too; in us the right feels and controls the left, the left the right, what we see is all inverted, and we are always in two minds.

Come dawn and cover me, come light and make me shade. From this razed place, erase me.

Life is death and death is life; to caress one is to embrace the other. Why, I have seen dead beasts, by mountain streams, by gas distended, quite pregnant with productive death. And you, my dear, you created our most fitting statement – though I could never say this to you, never hint that I even felt this way – by that one bloating of your own, when you gave birth, to death. (That we hid, that we did conceal, fearful for the only time of our closeness, threatened by all that we shared. It was after that still utterance of our love that you declined to articulate much else.)

Perhaps, my unfair fair one, you saw it clearer than the rest of us, and by never wanting to discover what we tried to find through you, knew it all the time, and so stayed true. Perhaps, however unjustly, your sex itself put you closer to what we,

276

denied or denying it, had to struggle for. Perhaps you alone saw our fate from the start, gender and proclivity equipping you to harbour conceptions we could not.

Some rain falls on me; I lick the moisture from my lips. As no hawk has come down to tear my bonds and no liberating soldiers attacked, I have had to relieve myself, standing here. Should I be ashamed? I am not. Water is most of what we are, and we ourselves are but bubbles, the body a temporary eddy, a standing wave in the stream of our aggregated course. We spend our most formative months aquatic, in a life that even then is loaned to us, an independence that from the start has strings attached, and whether our end is a composite unbinding or a binding decomposition, hardly matters. It is enough to walk this shore and scuff our way on sandy symbols without caring whether that strand strangles us.

Still, as the warmth cools upon my leg, I shiver, suddenly afraid, as though the repetition of this childhood action brings with it the fearfulness of childhood too, and I confess that, like a child, I cry. Ah, self-pity; I think we are at our most honest and sincere when we feel sorry for ourselves.

But my fear is most formality, my dear departed Sophist, a lip-service – trembling, I'll admit, not stiff – the body levies for itself, while the mind stays unastonished. And unconvinced that there is much reason to go on now apart from habit. If anything follows this existence, I might as well see it now rather than later, and if – as I suspect – the only meal that follows this aperitif is the little worms' feast, then why store up yet more coy memories to have to bid farewell when the inevitable comes round?

As for the vulgar interest in seeing our lives' continuing result – teasing out the present's knot a little further from the future, before it falls back into the past and tangles once again – I find no great compulsion to see for seeing's sake what I can't help but feel will still end up being more of the same. Every age, containing us, contains each other to the limit of our mutual understanding, and tomorrow, when it comes, will be but another day in a nearly endless procession of days upon days, and it will come and it will go, as all the rest have done and as we do too; for its own measure it will be, then for an infinitely longer time, not. And if we, swirled round inside that ever ebbing tide and sinking for our first and final time, are able to clutch at a few more of those straw days, I could believe that we do so not so much in the feeble expectation of saving ourselves, but more in the malicious hope of taking them down with us.

And what of superstition? The castle had a chapel once; our father, who is in the ground, had it excised. I stood, a young child, in the dim splendour of its window's great rosette, the day before the workmen came, crying at the thought of its removal, for purely sentimental reasons. Some days later, when that stained, dogmatic stillness had been removed, released from its metal sieve, I stood with you on the altar, blinking out at the living lushness of the summer countryside revealed.

The very intuition there must be something else beyond this physical world makes me guess it's wrong. We set ourselves up too thoroughly in this, and if we must indulge in such anthropopathism at all, why then I'd claim that reality could hardly miss a chance so tempting, and must feel duty-bound to let us down. The way things happen, just how they operate, includes an all-embracing brusqueness, an encompassing lack of ceremony and respect against which we can shore all our pious holdings and most cherished institutions and which we may rail against and oppose for exactly as long as we live, but which includes all our aspirations and degradations, all our promises and lies and all we do and all we don't, and which sweeps us in the end aside with less effort than metaphor can convey.

It takes more mistakes, more purely random chances, more chaos and irrelevance to produce the epic than the sordid yarn, or the hero than the common man. Romance, or our belief in it, is our genuine undoing.

Yet there is progress of a sort, I could admit; we once believed in happy hunting grounds, houris, real palaces and places in the sky, and man-shaped gods. Nowadays, amongst those with the wit to realise their predicament, a more sophisticated spirituality prevails; an infinite nonsensicalism replacing and displacing all, so that, one day, when all we here are dust, particle and wave-form, those who follow us will see just that as a deal more continuity than ever we deserved.

And within our little sphere, even mortality is mortal, and there is an end to endings, and the days; not endless.

By an unholy power, by itself meaningless, as senseless as it is implacable and irresistible coerced, we should know at last that all else but another knowing to consciousness is inimical, and that our love dies with us, not the reverse. (So long lives nothing, so long live nothing, so long.)

On the other hand, maybe it's just as they say.

But I doubt it, and I'll take my chances, like all else, with me.

The night points me at the earth-shadow cone's far point, as though to aim me at its farthest mark. Ah, discomfort me all you will, idiot star and accomplice rock. And, dark bird, do your most predictable, for what I've joined and what I've left, what I've done and what neglected, what I've felt and what dismissed, what I've been and what not been, matters and means, signifies and is less than one half thought in any one of us, and none the worse – and certainly none the better – for that.

Let me die, let me go; I've said my piece, refused to make it, and now – is that the dawn? Is this some sleep, or do I dream, or can I now hear reveille and the bugle's closing call? – I face my future, turn my back on a lifetime's desolation and on these dumb persecutors and am duly raised, brought up again, elevated glorious and triumphant to skies the colour of blood and roses, sneer at the dice that tumble (yes yes; die! die! *Iacta est alea*, we who are about to die despise you), laugh at cheers that rise, buoying me, and with that salute my end.